Copyright 2018 by Colin Hewitt

All rights reserved.

Cover photo by Luxorphoto/Shutterstock.com

No part of this book may be reproduced in any form or by any electronic or mechanical means, including information storage and retrieval systems, without permission in writing from the author. The only exception is by a reviewer, who may quote short excerpts in a review.

This book is a work of fiction. Names, characters, places, and incidents are either products of the author's imagination or are used fictitiously. Any resemblance to actual persons, living or dead, events, or locales is entirely coincidental.

Acknowledgments

First and foremost, I would like to say a huge thanks to my colleagues of the last thirty years -- well, from 1983 to 2013. You are still are my colleagues, and it goes without saying that I could not have written this book, nor, in all probability, survived without your help, your humour, forbearance, professionalism, and, most importantly, your support in the dark times that we all shared. It was a pleasure to have served with you.

A special mention must go to Peter Ritchie for his encouragement and his advice freely given, together with Mike Clague, Al Graham, Craig Fraser, Paul Ashworth, Brian Lile, Amy Burns, and Nick and Wendy Groome-Vine for their help when I needed a steer with some information.

Most of all to my wife, Carol, and our two great kids, Kathryn and Martin, for always being there for me.

Glossary

ABS - Acrylonitrile butadiene styrene. A hard plastic shell designed to prevent damage to contents

Alky - Alcoholic

ARV – Armed Response Vehicle

Aye – Scottish slang for "yes"

Baltic – Slang term for very cold

Bizzie – Slang term for Police Officer

CI – Chief Inspector

CID – Criminal Investigation Department

DCI – Detective Chief Inspector

DC – Detective Constable

DS – Detective Sergeant

DI – Detective Inspector

Fag - Cigarette

Flier – Slang term for being allowed home before stipulated finishing time

GMP – Greater Manchester Police

HB – Housebreaking; a burglary

HMRC – Her Majesty's Revenue and Customs; tax authority

Hen – Affectionate term for a woman/girl

Kip – Sleep

LIO – Local Intelligence Officer

OST – Officer Safety Training; Police self-defence tactics

Panda (Car) – A marked, uniformed officers' patrol vehicle

Piece Time – Refreshment break

Pished – Drunk

PF – Procurator Fiscal, the Scottish prosecuting authority

PC – Police Constable

POLSA – Police Search Advisor

PM – Post Mortem

Rat Shit – Small pieces of cannabis resin

Screw – To break into a house

Shufftie – To inspect or examine

Shug – Affectionate term for anyone named Hugh

UB – Uniform Branch; a uniformed Police Officer

Chapter One

The dark sleek shape slid over the wall and dropped into the shadows, still holding the strong plastic ABS double-shelled case, slightly larger than an attaché. Crouching low against the foot of the wall, he remained hidden in the darkness of the shadows cast by the street lights, waiting a few minutes to allow his eyes to become accustomed to the darkness.

Presently, the outline of the ground around him, the rise and fall of its undulations, became visible to him as he moved off, slowly at first, ensuring that he made no sound, and then broke into a steady jog at a pace that he knew he could keep to and where his breathing was deep and regular.

Running up the incline of around 200 yards in the darkness of the November evening, he could hear his breathing and see his breath against the cold air in the moonlight. The only other sound heard was the soft crunch of the frost under his boots as he made his way towards the woods. He didn't look back, as he knew from his previous reconnaissance that he might be visible from the street and his night vision would be compromised by the street lights, having to be adjusted again.

Pressing onwards, he jogged into the woods and began tracking northwards towards the other side, zig-zagging between and around the trees, ducking low as limbs came into view, but allowing the smaller branches to brush against the black cotton of his boiler suit, over which he was wearing a pair of black combat trousers with two sizeable pockets on the outside of his thighs. The carrying case was held low to the ground at all times to make sure that it didn't knock against any objects unnecessarily.

After about five minutes, he reached the far side of the woods and stopped. Stepping off the small track that had been carved out by many dog walkers over the years, he knew this would be the most difficult part of his journey. Squatting down low in the undergrowth, he paused for a few minutes and listened for anything that might indicate he was not alone. He was aware that local youngsters frequented the area when they were looking for a quiet place to go drinking and, even more frequently, that joy riders on stolen motorcycles or dirt bikes went tearing around the fields, scrambling up the hill in front of him, well out of the way of, and inaccessible to, the police from the local station.

The hill below him was bordered at the bottom by a small burn and by a railway line, built up on an embankment that formed part of the south suburban line. It had once carried thousands of passengers around Edinburgh but had now been consigned to history by Mr Beeching after his major cull of the railways in the 1960s. It was now seldom used and only for freight transporting.

To his left, the line swept westwards in a lazy curve towards the bridge at a major road junction, and then northwards towards the city centre. In the distance, on the far side of the railway line, he could see the playing fields of the university and, to the right, his target. Satisfied that he was alone, he stood up and set off again down the hill, keeping to the same steady pace as before and keenly aware that momentum might increase his speed.

He ran towards the bottom of the hill, still keeping as low a profile as possible, listening intently for any sounds out of the ordinary as he moved and quickly covered the 500-or-so yards. Upon reaching the bottom, he stopped short of the burn and grabbed his wire cutters from his pocket. Wading into the burn, he crossed quickly. The cold water was a shock, but it was shallow and only two or three feet across. He could have jumped the burn with a short run up but that would have left a very obvious indication that he had been there, and he didn't want that.

He now reached into his other pocket and took out a head torch, which he had already covered in black insulating tape so as to allow only a small, concentrated beam of light to be projected. Placing the bands around his head, he stood up and, keeping his face to the ground, turned on the head torch. He snipped through the chain link fence in front of him at waist-height, cutting in a straight line downwards. This took only a few minutes, but the cut he made at right angles took a few more.

Bending back the wire, he moved through the hole created and, once on the inside, he reached up to his forehead to turn off the torch. He then moved as quickly and as silently as possible to his right, keeping to the shadows of the embankment and trying to minimise the noise from the railway ballast stones crunching under his feet.

After a few hundred yards, he noticed a large gap in the fence that dirt bikers had obviously created, but it was something that he had missed previously. There was also a small ford that they had constructed with a few large stones and lots of the ballast from the embankment.

Pausing briefly, he looked back up the hill and surveyed the scene. A lot of large bushes and undergrowth grew on the far side of the burn, but there was a tell-tale sign of motor bike tracks, well-worn into the grass, especially at this time of the year. These bushes had blocked the view of his previous surveillance, and he knew that he had made a mistake.

"Fuck!" he hissed under his breath, annoyed at his obvious error, but there was nothing he could do about it now. He had a schedule to keep. He looked back over his shoulder, and then he was jogging again towards his predetermined vantage point. After a few minutes and another few hundred yards, he put down the ABS case and climbed the embankment, looking over. In front of him he saw the target – the old folk's home, or retirement complex, as they were known these days. He was there. He checked his watch – time enough -- and he knew his target would be leaving shortly, certainly before eight o'clock.

He scrambled back down the embankment and recovered his attaché case. With his face to the ground once more, he turned on the head torch again and clicked open the case, having previously set the combination locks to save time. Opening it up, he took out the butt section of the Blaser R8 .308 rifle and then the barrel. Inverting the stock section, he placed the barrel into the slot and tightened the two hexagonal locking screws, already in place within the butt section, with the Allen key provided and adjusted it to the desired finger tension. The breech section slotted straight in, as did the trigger-magazine assembly, both clicking home without difficulty. The Zeiss Diavari 26 x 72 telescopic sight clicked home in a similar fashion. With the bipod attaching to the small protrusion under the barrel, he inserted the magazine and drew back the bolt, sliding a round into the breach. He was now ready.

Turning off the torch again, he scrambled back up the embankment with the rifle, where he took up a comfortable position, lying prone with his body short of the rail nearest to him. He tried to leave the ballast as undisturbed as possible, resting his elbows on the sleepers supporting the railway line and spreading his legs out behind him. This, he knew, would ensure that he had a stable base for the shot he was about to take. The legs of the bi-pod were positioned over the rail, also resting on the sleepers, but he held the rifle clear of the rail, tight into his shoulder. Looking through the sight he could clearly see the gable-end of the old folks home and the side door that was situated there outlined against the street lights. The magnification brought the target so close that he felt he could almost reach out and touch it, but it was, in fact, just over 500 yards away.

He checked his watch again.

Won't be long now, he thought and then returned to his view through the sight. He maintained this position for what seemed like a lifetime -- kind of ironic, he thought, as he was about to end one – and then the reason for him being there came into view.

His target had just walked out the door at the gable end of the single-storied, L-shaped building, where he stopped to light a cigarette, as he always did. Smoking wasn't allowed in the home and smokers needed their fix as soon as they could get it after a period of abstention. From his position, the shooter watched as the target pulled on his cigarette and inhaled deeply.

Smoking will kill you, mate, he thought, but then he had been responsible for more deaths, more misery and hardship than anyone else he knew. The drugs that he supplied through his networks and the constant fight to maintain those networks, the violence and intimidation, the beatings and destruction, had caused many, many more people to be hurt, either deliberately or by being caught up in the crossfire.

Remembering his training – breathing, stance and position, trigger action, sight picture, all elements of good shooting practise -- the shooter took up the slack on the trigger. With the crosshairs sighted on the middle of the target's chest, the shot, when it rang out, almost took the shooter by surprise. This was also a good sign. The sound moderator had done its job, minimising the crack of the shot, but not completely. The 150-grain soft-point round left the muzzle of the rifle at 2800 feet per second and covered the intervening distance in a fraction of that, where it tore into the target's chest with a *whack,* creating a devastating wound channel as it mushroomed on contact. The flattened-out round immediately caused massive trauma to his lungs, heart, and spine, and although it had been slowed down considerably, the bullet still passed through his body, hurling him backwards and taking him off his feet. He was dead before he hit the ground.

Remaining on target just long enough to see the round strike home and the target fall, the shooter didn't eject the spent shell casing, choosing to keep it within the breech of the rifle. There was no sense in leaving any evidence. The target had been very aware of police surveillance, but then, so was the shooter, and he knew that he was now a hunted man, and not just by the police. He had to create distance from where he was right now. The greater the distance, the better.

He scrambled back down the embankment and quickly disassembled the Blaser, placing each component back in its pre-formed foam position by touch. He closed the case, and then he was off and running again back along the fence line, where he ducked through the gap created by the joy riders and their ford.

Keeping to the worn tracks as best he could, he ran down the far side of the burn until he reached a small bridge, which gave access to the fields for the farmer. He had thought about running through the water, but his research had shown that that would not put off any dog that might be sent after him right now. Police dogs followed and tracked by scent trails given off by grass or undergrowth that had been compressed underfoot, but they could also follow an air scent trail. They would need to be right on his tail to do that, though.

No point in taking that chance, he thought, although he was confident that he hadn't been seen. He ran through ankle-deep sticky mud mixed in with sheep shit that had been deposited around a water trough and livestock feeding station, before heading southwards over the field again, keeping to the dark shadow cast by the factory on the front street. As he glanced to his right, he saw the small wood he had jogged through some fifteen or twenty minutes before and, as he ran, he listened for any signs of people.

Circling to his right, he skirted the incline he had run up and kept to the flat ground as his breathing was becoming laboured and heavy with the pace he was setting. He reached the barbed-wire fence over to his left after about ten minutes, just as he had planned.

Not bad for one and a half miles, carrying a weapon, he said to himself.

As he reached the farmer's track at a side entrance to the field, he saw the five-bar gate he was looking for with its hard-core entrance. He then became aware of a cacophony of noise around him and looked back to where he had come from. In the distance, over by the Shopping Centre and adjacent park, the firework display had started. He saw that the clouds of cordite and gunpowder smoke from the pyrotechnic explosions were drifting in his direction. Pieces of cardboard that had housed the firework shells would start landing in the field due to wind drift and that, he hoped, would also mask his exit. That, and time.

The track he was standing on, he knew, was seldom used and only then by courting couples parked up in their cars, or by joyriders and thieves intent on burning out the car they had stolen. He leapt over the gate and continued running to a small branch-off on the left where he had parked his car. Moving quickly to the rear offside tyre, he reached up under the wheel arch to a small hook he had had welded there and retrieved the keys. He threw the Blaser case onto the passenger seat, climbed in, started up the engine, and drove off.

He glanced at the clock on the dashboard. It said 20.05 hours as he drove to the end of the hard-core track and turned onto the tarmac. He drove quickly but within the speed limits for a short time and then joined the main carriageway shortly thereafter. Within fifteen minutes, he was at his safe house, where he parked the car in the garage near the house. He transferred the Blaser case to the boot of the car, locked it, and then locked up the garage.

There's a lot of criminals about, he thought wryly, before walking to another car.

Taking off his boots and combat over-trousers, he placed them in a plastic bag and then threw them into the boot before driving home. He needed a shower badly and, besides, he had to go to work in the morning. He knew he would be busy.

With a little luck, he had just started a war.

Chapter Two

Iris Harper was pushing sixty years old and had been a care assistant for many years. She enjoyed her work, looking after the people she now considered to be her friends. The job suited her down to the ground as she lived only a short distance away from the Craigmillar Retirement Home. She knew that she was well thought of by the home's management team and was trusted with responsibility, despite her lack of formal qualifications.

But it was time for a smoke break, and she had gone out the kitchen door at the rear of the home with a single cigarette and her lighter. As she did so, the passive infrared light sensor snapped on and the glaring light illuminated the wheelie bins and recycling containers that were parked there. She lit up knowing that she was desperately trying to stop, or at least cut down, on the amount that she smoked and figured that not bringing the packet with her would help.

It had been a long day, a double shift, and now, towards the end of her shift, when most of the residents had begun to get settled down for the night, she knew she would be handing over her duties shortly when the night shift came on. Strolling away from the harsh glare of the lamp, holding her coat closed against the cold night air, she turned the corner at the side of the building where one of the fire escape doors was situated and saw a horrendous sight, made worse by the clouds of smoke billowing past the building, just like a scene from a horror film.

The body of Matty Buchan was lying on his back in a large pool of blood. His arms were splayed out wide, almost like a crucifix, and his legs were positioned with one under the other, nearly cross-legged. His mouth was agape, almost in surprise, with a cigarette butt stuck to his lower lip. His cigarette had burned down with the ash still hanging in place due to the lack of wind in the lea of the building. His heavy Barbour jacket was open and a large, bloody mass of gore was spread out over his shirt. Of course, she would not remember these details as the shock of what she had discovered kicked in.

"Oh my God!" she shouted out at no one in particular.

She quickly carried on around to the front door and rushed inside, still holding her cigarette, shouting, "Call the Police! Call the Police!" having completely forgotten about the "No Smoking" rule. A colleague joined her as she grabbed the nearest phone and dialled treble nine, asking the call handler for an ambulance.

"What's wrong, Iris? What's happened?" a colleague asked her.

"There's a bloke lying dead out there in the car park! There's blood everywhere!" she blurted out, gulping in air as her heart pumped furiously.

As the ambulance call handler came on the line, Iris jabbered incoherently, trying to pass all the details of what she had seen at once. The call handler, attempting unsuccessfully to interrupt her and calm her down, tried to elicit the information she required. Allowing her to finish, she calmly asked for her name.

"Iris Harper," she replied.

"What number are you calling from? I can see that you're on a landline. Can you just confirm the number?" Iris did so.

"Where is the injured party?" the call handler asked.

"He's lying in the car park at the side of the care home," she responded.

"Is the injured party breathing?"

"Oh, I couldn't tell you, Hen. I never really looked that close. I got such a fright, with all the blood and that."

"So, the injured party is bleeding?"

"Aye, Hen. There's a right lot of blood that he's lying in. An awful lot."

"Are you with the injured party right now," the call handler asked, "and have you checked to see if there is pulse?"

"No. I'm not with him right now. I came back into the home to get a phone," Iris replied.

"I'm just going to put you on hold for a couple of seconds. I'm going to get an ambulance to you as soon as I can. Please stay on the line, Iris. I'll be back quickly."

"Aye. Okay, Hen."

After a few moments, the call handler came back to her as she had promised.

"I've got an ambulance on its way, Iris. Could you go back to the casualty and begin CPR? I'll stay on the phone and talk you through it," the call handler asked.

"I can go back to him, but I don't think I can do CPR, Hen," she replied.

"That's okay, Iris" the call handler responded, "That's okay. I understand. The ambulance crew will be with you shortly."

As she left the building to go to where Matty was lying, other members of staff had also gone out to see what had happened, and she then heard the tell-tale sounds of two-tone sirens as the ambulance left the south-side depot, only a short distance away.

On first sight, the ambulance crew knew that this was a lost cause. The amount of blood was a good indication of the severity of the injuries. Nevertheless, they checked for a pulse on Matty's outstretched wrist, without success. They then cut open Matty's shirt and saw the gaping hole in Matty's chest, almost in the centre and both immediately thought *"gunshot wound."* Their observations and information were radioed back to the control room, asking that the police should attend. They attached the electrodes of their heart monitoring equipment around the wound as best they could, still looking for a pulse and continued working on him as the first police officers arrived, having already been informed.

The first officers on the scene were of a like mind with their ambulance colleagues – this was a lost cause. Almost immediately, one of PCs was on the radio back to his control room, "Double One to Alpha."

"Go ahead AM11," the controller responded using the NATO phonetic alphabet.

"This looks suspicious. Very suspicious. Can you have the Sergeant and Inspector attend here as soon as possible please? Better get the CID, too. We have a body with a large chest wound . . . so far?" He spoke into the radio, finishing with a question designed to ensure that the controller had managed to note all the details passed to that point.

"So far," the controller agreed.

"The injured party is in the car park at the Peffermill Old Folks Home. There's a lot of blood. The ambulance crew can't find any signs of life, although they're still trying. One of them mentioned a possible gunshot injury. Can I have more officers attend the scene? We'll have to keep the area clear. We might need the ARV informed, too."

The control room, always busy even on quiet nights, complied immediately with the requests, making phone calls and passing radio messages back and forth on differing channels. The control room inspector weighed up the information available at that time and decided to authorise the Armed Response Vehicle to draw their firearms from the on-board safe. A dedicated operator was nominated to this incident and its content was then blocked on the computer system to prevent every police officer in the Force from looking at the details.

Despite how busy the police were, with call after call to assist the Fire Services who were coming under attack from local youths when they tried to put out their bonfires, very soon resources were dispatched from all over the city and the well-oiled, practised, and slick procedures kicked into gear. As support arrived, the senior uniform officer present delegated duties to ensure the area was kept clear. The details of people who had been at or near the body were recorded, as were the ambulance staff, the first officers on scene, and other staff within the home. With the arrival of the first CID officer on scene, the on-call senior detectives were dispatched or made aware of what was happening, depending on their rank, and call-outs for the Identification Branch officers were authorised.

After an hour or so, a crime scene manager was nominated, with the resources present complying with her instructions, despite the competing priorities of their respective parts in the incident. A formal log was started and updated from officers' notebooks; others were tasked with making initial door-to-door enquiries locally in an attempt to gather any information regarding what might have happened. This was done with the firearms officers giving a visible support in case anything untoward was accidently stumbled upon.

This was "the golden hour," when vital evidence could be secured and re-visited at a later date and time if need be.

Later that night, about a half hour before he was due to start, Hugh Collins parked his car at the police headquarters. Having first swiped his dual purpose warrant card at the barrier, under the watchful eye of CCTV cameras, Collins entered the staff car park. Access to the staff car park was limited due to over subscription by the bosses that worked there during the day. They all wanted a space that they thought their rank deserved, but at night there was no problem. Walking athletically and purposely across the car park past the traffic department, he glanced over and noted that both Armed Response Vehicles were not parked up in their usual position at the front of a queue of traffic cars and motorbikes.

Hmm, he thought, *must be out on a job.*

Wandering into the porta cabin that served as the ARV locker room where most of the troops could keep their equipment – ballistic helmet, goggles (that made them look like tank commanders from WW2), baseball cap, boiler suit (for their training days), along with gloves, snoods, sidearm holster with ammunition pouches attached for spare magazines, and, of course, ballistic body armour that was a bastard to wear at the best of times -- he was taking off his jeans and putting on his combat trousers when Jamie Beattie, his partner, walked in.

"Hey there, Shug," he boomed, and then, "Sleep well?"

"Nah. Not really. But hopefully we'll get a wee kip tonight," he laughed in response.

The pair of them chewed the fat as they got dressed, flinging their body armour over their heads but not tucking in the front plate or zipping it up. No sense in getting uncomfortable this early in the day, or night, as was the case. Besides, they hadn't even had a brew yet – nobody started their work without a cup of tea or coffee, did they? As they crossed the car park again, they threw their equipment bags on the ground adjacent to the parking space where the back shift would normally park up the vehicle.

As they walked into the office, the back shift traffic control room operator shouted at them, "Don't get comfy, boys. There's been a shooting in Craigmillar. You'd better get up to the Ops Room and see the Inspector."

"Bollocks," they muttered, almost in unison, but they decided they'd better find out what was going on and quickly made their way up to the Force control room in the main building.

The Operations Room was laid out in three or four separate workstations, each of which consisted of large banks of computer screens and terminals, where two or three operators constantly created, updated, and closed off incidents as they were created or finalised. Each wore headsets so that when communicating with officers on the ground, they would have both hands free to type up the information passed.

Around the walls of the Ops Room were yet more banks of screens relaying live coverage of the many CCTV cameras dotted around Edinburgh city centre and out into the counties. Set back from the rest of the congregation was the "top table," where the officer in charge sat, usually an Inspector.

"What's up in Craigmillar, Boss?" Collins asked as they approached the table.

"Right, then," Willie Dunn said, taking a deep breath and reclining in his chair. Inspector Dunn had seen and done it all in his time in the job. Nearing the end of his service, he was exactly the type of boss most cops loved – laid back, unflappable, and decisive. He was known as a man who would never ask anyone to do something he wouldn't do. The troops knew that he had their backs at all times, as he had completed most of his time on the streets as an operational cop and sergeant and knew the pressures that officers worked under. Very little took him by surprise these days.

"There's been a shooting – we think, anyway -- at the Peffermill Old Folks Home," he began. "There's one dead and, at this stage, we don't know who he is or what it's about. Both ARVs are off at the locus. We've been phoning the bosses most of the last few hours and a murder enquiry is being set up. They want you guys to get your arses down there and take over from the backshift. I'll make arrangements to get you transport there. They can bring the backshift here when they're ready. Is there any reason that you cannot carry a firearm tonight?" This last question was always asked by the Ops Room Inspector as a preamble to firearms officers being authorised to carry weapons. The answers were invariably negative, but it had to be asked in case they had been drinking or had anything going on in their lives that could affect their judgement or mental faculties.

Collins and Beattie each said "No" in their turn and then, without reference to the idiot card he had been given a long time before, Willie Dunn went into his oft repeated statement, "An officer is not entitled to open fire against a person unless the officer has reasonable grounds for believing that that person is committing, or is about to commit, an action likely to endanger the life, or cause serious injury, to the officer or any other person and there is no other way of preventing that danger. That is the law. Remember your training." All three then made a notebook entry that they had delivered and accepted the warning and noted the time. In the officers' case, they used their fancy new electronic notebooks. Dunn just used his old paper one.

"Head back to the Link. There's a car coming in to get you," he said.

"Will do, Boss," Collins said, and they were off, heading out down the stairs again.

"And for fuck's sake, be safe," Dunn shouted after them, before returning to his computer terminal.

On arrival after the fast drive to the locus, Collins and Beattie sought out the crime scene manager, Laura Fraser, a Detective Sergeant, hugely respected with great experience.

"Hi Laura. We're the nightshift. What do you want us to do?" Collins asked of his former shift teammate.

"Hi there, Shug. Long time, no see," she responded, giving him a hug before quickly bringing them up to speed with what she knew at that time.

"We need a firearms presence at the front and back of the locus in case anything is found or stumbled over, probably overnight, just for contingencies," she continued.

"Who's the body?" Collins asked her

"We think that it's Matty Buchan. A couple of the local UB lads know him, but that's not confirmed yet," she replied.

Collins and Beattie acknowledged their instructions and then contacted their backshift colleagues to find out where they were. A few minutes later, they all met up at one of the parked up ARVs, where the backshift unloaded their Heckler & Koch G36 carbines and then their H & K 9mm Glock sidearms, pointing the muzzles into a ballistic bag, just in case of any stupidity – and it had happened before -- where someone had left a round in the breech before easing the springs of the weapon by pulling the trigger . . . and testing the bag! Collins and Beattie counted the rounds in the magazines now on board the car, checked the equipment and, when satisfied all was present and correct, said goodnight to their backshift colleagues and loaded up themselves. Returning to see Laura Craig, Beattie spoke up first.

"That's us ready to go, Laura. Where do you want us?"

"Right then, lads" he said, "Dick Neilson's the SIO. He's been speaking with the other bosses and, like I said, they want the firearms to stay, just in case. It's looking like the culprit has come over the back way anyway – nobody's seen or heard a thing at the front, as far as we can tell so far. Can you guys get to the back of the home on the other side of the fence?"

"Is that Dick 'The Prick' Neilson?" Collins asked, his heart sinking.

"Aye, that's him."

"Dick by name, Dick by nature. Every fucking time there's a shite detail that I'm on, he's behind it," Collins stated in a matter-of-fact way, thoughts of his previous dealings flashing through his memory.

"Yeah, I know," Laura replied, "I've asked for a van to be brought up with some grub and a brew later. Hopefully, that'll happen."

"Anywhere we should avoid, apart from the obvious?" Collins enquired.

"Not really. The back needs covered, though," Laura responded, before they moved off as they had been instructed.

Collins and Beattie moved to the rear of the old folk's home with a couple of unarmed uniform colleagues. Neither of them saw the point in this as the culprit was long gone, but said nothing and did as they were told. Besides, the newspapers were not above sneaking photos of a crime scene, even from far away. They had both been through this before in their years in the police and with the firearms department, and they each knew that their equipment and clothing were of a far better standard than their uniformed colleagues'. A small comfort, but at least Collins knew he was warm with his Arktis coat and thermal layering under his body armour, his combat trousers did not leech warmth from his legs, and his Altberg boots kept his feet well-insulated.

Collins could make out the outline of the railway and, as he made his way towards the embankment, he decided to pass the time as best he could. He knew that he would have to stay focussed. He had seen the results of bored cops many times and, with his unarmed colleague, went for a walk over the field towards the railway line, through where it had been broken down, chatting as they went, introducing themselves to each other.

"This is going to be a long night, Jim," Collins said to the young cop he was paired with, "but at least is not raining."

"Yeah, I know. And it's the last one, and we'll be back on days after," Jim Hay responded.

"Aye, I know. But you'll probably be back here then, as well. This enquiry's going to take a while, especially with Dick Neilson in charge."

"How's that?" Jim asked. "I've only just started. This is my first big incident. I've only got six months of service."

"Ah, you're just out the wrapper, then? Well, a post-mortem will have to be done, probably in the morning but, right now, we'll have to keep the area sterile so that every piece of evidence or whatever is thought to be important, is recovered. The cordon will stay put until daylight and then the search teams will come in and do a fingertip search of the car park, to start with. They'll probably go further as more information comes to light. So that'll take some time," Collins explained, "and then there's going to be door-to-door enquiries again, maybe even a house-to-house. The ballistics experts will work out their angles and stuff like that to tell us where the shot came from. They're going to have to find the round that killed him first, of course."

"Who's Dick Neilson?" Jim asked, innocently.

"Him and I go back a long way. He's the man in charge. He talks a great game but doesn't produce one. In my opinion, for what that's worth, is that he's a crap boss, not because he makes bad decisions. He's a crap boss because he can't make *any* decisions."

Collins had already realised that a large capacity bullet had been used and, judging by the injuries Laura had described, he figured that someone must have used a large calibre weapon, a rifle of some sort, taking the shot from some distance away. He and his colleague wandered over to the fence line and saw a gap in the fence with tyre tracks going through. Walking through, he climbed up the embankment onto the railway line but stopped.

"Better not. Not sure how many trains use this line anymore. Don't want to get run over and chuffed to bits," he said to Jim, chuckling to himself.

From where he was standing, he noted that the railway line would have given a perfect line of sight towards the side exit from the old folk's home.

"Well, Jim," he said to his young colleague, "if I was going to shoot someone from a distance, I'd've done it from about here. Maybe further along the line," pointing with the barrel of his H & K carbine.

"I don't know much about firearms at all, Shug," Jim replied. "How long you been doing it?"

"I've been in for eighteen years now and have done the firearms for about five or six years. I do the public order, officer's safety training, and I'm search-trained, too. Much better than office work, in my opinion. I've always been into the hunting, shooting, and fishing. As a matter of fact, I was out earlier last night, shooting some vermin."

"Who's been shot?"

"A guy called Matty Buchan. One of the big players in the drug trade in the city. There are a few, right enough, but the secret squirrel boys have never been able to really nail him."

"How that?" Jim came back right away.

"Oh, he's a smart cookie -- or was. We've never found him with his drugs on him or in his house. He's got loads of contacts all over, very conscious of surveillance, CCTV at his house, rarely uses mobiles and never writes anything down. He has to remember it all -- all the payoffs, who owes him what, et cetera. He's got a couple of businesses in other peoples' names supplying doormen at nightclubs, car washes, or laundrettes and such like."

"He's never been lifted, like?"

"He's been lifted a good few times, but not for drugs. If you get a conviction for dealing, they'll come after you for the money you make. And it's up to him to prove that it's legit to get it back; not us to prove its dirty money," Collins replied, continuing, "He's been done with assaults loads of times, some quite serious, attempted murders, really. And he really is off his head. Apparently he was diagnosed psychopathic, sociopathic or something like that. You have to be a loony to know a loony, if you ask me. A scary bloke."

"I'm just into the job and everyone I have dealings with seems scary, especially around here," Jim said, slightly embarrassed.

"You'll get used to that, Jim. But he's a seriously scary individual and, funnily enough, he comes from money, went to private school, nice folks and family life, the whole nine yards. Family disowned him when he went off the rails as a teenager, seemingly, after he went to a trick cyclists. Maybe wasn't breastfed enough as a child…?" Collins allowed himself to trail off, sensing that he might be placing doubts in the young man's head regarding his career choice

"But this is a great job. Not what we're doing right now, right enough. You'll see and do things that you'll never do anywhere else. Some good, some bad, but you'll have fun along the way. "

"How do you know all this?"

"Getting out on the street. I used to work near here and it was the same there. Nobody tells you anything unless you've got them by the balls and, even then, sometimes they just take it on the chin. That, and reading the intelligence about folk in your area, who's doing what, that type of thing. With the bad guys that the firearms and search teams have to deal with, it's best to know and keep up to date." Collins lit up a small cheroot cigar and puffed on it. "And always remember: When you're marching, you're not fighting. We're still getting paid, hopefully some food and a brew will come our way and, at the very least, we're going home in the morning. Unlike some," pointing back towards the old folk's home, with a smirk on his face.

Chapter Three

Richard Neilson had taken the phone call from his boss, Detective Superintendent McInnes, at a late hour the previous evening telling him that there had been a murder in Edinburgh's south side. He had gulped, hoping that his boss at the other end of the line had not picked up on it. Neilson had always been plagued by self-doubt, something that he had done well to cover up in his rise through the ranks, but he knew what was coming next.

"You'll be leading a seasoned team of detectives, Dick. A good team. I'll keep an oversight, of course, but your deputy is Willie Stuart. There'll be a post-mortem in the morning at about eight, I think, at the city mortuary. We couldn't get two doctors to do it during the night. I'm about to phone Willie and tell him. Can you get to Craigmillar early, say, by six, so that you can have a look at the locus and set the wheels in motion for what has to be done?

"Yes, surely," he replied. "Who's at the scene right now?"

"Laura Fraser's there just now. She's done a good job so far as I can make out. She'll more than likely still be there when you arrive."

"Do we know who's been killed or how it came about?"

"Initial enquiries say it's Matty Buchan. That's still to be confirmed. It's looking like a shooting. There's no point in speculating right now. As you know, there's so many people up and down the country who could've done it."

"No problem there, then. I've never heard of him" Neilson replied, almost immediately kicking himself for showing his lack of criminal intelligence knowledge to his superior. "But I'll be there at six and take it from there."

As he hung up the phone, his mind began to turn over, running through what he should and shouldn't do, what he could do, what he must do, and how he would go about it. He had spent most of his seventeen years' service in office-based support work or in various squads working eight to four, Monday to Friday, which he knew he was good at. He had managed to be promoted three times, after all.

Nevertheless, he spent a very restless, almost sleepless, night and was awake long before his alarm went off at five am. After a shower and a shave, he dressed and climbed into his car, arriving just before six am. Walking into the station, he followed the signs to the CID offices and walked in to find no one there.

"They're out at the crime scene, Boss," a voice said to him after a few moments. As he turned around, a balding, heavily built but nonetheless athletic-looking man, approached him with his hand outstretched.

"Willie Stuart," he said, introducing himself.

"Ah, right. I'm DCI Richard Neilson."

No shit, Sherlock, Stuart thought as they shook hands.

Neither had met before, but each knew the other by reputation and Stuart fitted his well, Neilson thought, which his immaculate suit, shirt, and contrasting tie, with a little fag ash on the lapel indicated. Detective Inspector Stuart was highly regarded as a meticulous, if unconventional officer, whose laid-back manner hid an intelligent and serious-minded individual. Although not university educated, he was, nonetheless, known to be very well-read.

Stuart saw a slightly built but fit looking man, with eyes that gazed straight at him giving nothing away and who was also known for having a meticulous demeanour, especially when it came to paperwork, but who had a habit of taking credit for others' hard work.

"Let's grab a radio and get to the locus, Boss. I've got a grab bag from the divisional officers in case we need anything when we're down there," he said. Willie Stuart, Neilson would soon find out, was a no-nonsense, up-front, old-school detective and not a man for formalities.

"Grab bag?" Neilson asked, trying not to appear slow on the uptake.

"Aye, you know, paper, pens, bags, swabs, gloves. That sort of thing."

"Oh, yes, of course," he agreed, as he followed his DI out to the car.

They didn't say much to each other on the short drive to the locus. Neither had had a coffee yet nor slept too well. In Willie Stuarts' case, it was because he'd been at a retirement doo and was now meant to be on a day off. He'd had a few drinks, but when he had taken the call from McInnes, he knew he would have to call it a night earlier than planned.

On arrival, they parked up short of the cordon that two uniformed officers were manning. Blue incident tape had been strung across the street and a panda car was parked up in the middle of the road with its engine running. One officer was in the vehicle and the other standing beside it, the blue lights flashing, as the street had been closed and it was still dark.

As they made their way towards the officers, they were recognised and allowed to pass with the merest hint of a head nod in acknowledgement from Neilson. Willie Stuart, however, said, "Thanks lads. Hope it wasn't too long a night for you? Did you get a break?" remembering the many times when he had been in uniform and had done the same thing.

"Yeah, we did, thanks," the older of the cops responded. "The van's just up around the corner."

They walked on. Neilson was looking to see where he was going, but Stuart was looking around to see what types of buildings were there; what types of houses there were and if they looked occupied; if there were any shops about that might have CCTV footage onto the street; if the factory was open and might it have shift workers?

They soon met up with Laura Fraser who looked remarkably fresh and attractive despite having been working all night and most of the previous evening, too. After Stuart had introduced Neilson to her, Laura began her handover briefing.

"Right, then. Where to begin?" she started. "We think the deceased is Matty Buchan. He didn't have any ID on him but a couple of the local lads think that it's him. It seems he came to visit his old mum in the home last night. He hasn't signed in on the register, though, but it appears he's a regular visitor once or twice a week. His mum's eighty-nine and has dementia, but the staff know him as her son. I've got a list of residents and staff somewhere for you. Not all were on duty last night, of course. I think we know about Matty falling out with his family a good few years ago?"

She glanced up at both men and then continued, "Seems he doesn't stick to the rules when he visits. He goes in the front door but leaves by side doors; the fire alarm is always going off. We think he's gone out the side door at the gable-end of the building and walked into somebody who's shot him. Not from close range, though."

"Walked into somebody," Neilson interrupted, "but not at close range? What do you mean?"

"Well, I don't mean that he's literally bumped into someone. I mean that someone has been waiting for him in the car park, close by or somewhere near. Near enough to shoot him. He was found a few feet from the fire escape, just at the corner of the building. It seems to be a large calibre bullet, and it's made a right mess of him."

"Could someone have come from the street?" Neilson asked.

"Anything is possible right now, Boss," she replied, glancing in Willie Stuarts' direction, just as she caught him in mid eye-roll. Stifling a smile, she carried on. "He's been shot from the front, in the chest. There's blood spattering on the gable-end of the building going in the direction of the front street. Someone could've been hiding, I suppose, yes." Neilson merely nodded, before Laura continued.

"He was found by an Iris Harper who works in the home. She had gone out for a fag just after eight pm. She called the ambulance. The times will be on the log. They've attended along with uniform cops but it was a hopeless task. The ambulance men noted a time of death as 20.15 hours, but he was dead before that. The PM will give an accurate time of death and the cause."

"But he was shot, you said?" Neilson chipped in again.

"Aye, we know that but we will still have to know definitively what killed him," Stuart interjected. "We'll have to prove everything." Stuart looked at Laura with another rolling of his eyes.

"Anyway, two of the lads went with him to the mortuary when he was taken away." She glanced up again from her notes with a look as if she was asking if either had any questions and then carried on.

"The Identification Branch attended after the call out. They've done their full 360-degree video recording, still pictures, et cetera, et cetera. They bagged his hands and feet so that we can do the wet and dry swabs later. Fingernail scrapings were done, entry logs done, initial door-to-door was done but doesn't seem to have turned up much, if anything. There was a night shift in the factory just along the road but nothing seen or heard. That'll have to be checked again. We've had a look for any CCTV, but there's only the bike shop along the road, and the university grounds. They might have CCTV and maybe their security patrols popped by. However, with the firework display last night in the Inch Park, there would've been a lot of noise and smoke from that." She again stopped and took a swig from her lukewarm coffee,

"The firearms were here last night, just in case, and were stood down a short time ago. The search teams will be coming on as soon as they can see what they're looking at. Not sure who the POLSA will be. The admin departments are aware, or will be shortly, that we'll need to cover the cordon for the foreseeable future. They'll get the uniform troops for you. That's me. I don't think I've missed anything?"

"Seems you've got the bases covered, Laura." Stuart said. "I think you need your bed."

"Well, you're the old detective. Is it just a hunch?" she chided him. "I'll hang around until my relief gets here and hand over to him."

"Let's take a look," Stuart said to Neilson as they walked away from the van towards the crime scene. They were a few yards away when Laura shouted, "Willie, can I have a quick word before I go?"

Turning to her, he walked back a few steps and noticed she was holding her hand up flat out towards him, with her index finger pointing over his shoulder.

"I'll catch you up, Boss" he said to Neilson, catching Laura's drift and then, walking back to Laura again, said, "Aye, what is it?" in quieter tones.

"What the fuck is he doing here, Willie? He couldn't solve crime if you gave him all the evidence in the world and a signed confession."

"I know, I know, but the decision has been made higher up. How a guy who's been in an office all his life can make a CI, let alone a DCI, I'll never know."

"Isn't he the one who left post-it notes on stuff he thought important at an attempted murder scene a few years ago when he was a sergeant"

"I haven't heard that one, but I could believe it. He seems to be like a rabbit caught in the headlights. Get away home, Laura, and get some kip. If I need any more info, I'll give you a bell later in the day."

With that, he walked quickly back to where Neilson was standing. "All okay, Willie?" he asked.

"Laura was just reminding me about the next of kin need to be told once we know who the deceased actually is," he lied and, with no response coming from Neilson, they walked on into the car park of the old folks home.

Stuart placed his hands in his trouser pockets, an old habit that he had acquired over the years in order to stop him touching things or picking up anything. *Maybe something you should do,* he thought about saying to Neilson as they walked to survey the crime scene.

The car park was about forty-square-yards with spaces marked for parking. There were flower beds situated around an outer low-level wall but with little growing in them at this time of year. The main door was in the corner of the single-storeyed, L-shaped building with a foyer and a register for visitors to sign in, to comply with fire regulations, immediately behind the door. The home had thirty rooms for residents, although not all were occupied, they would later find out. The kitchens were to the rear with a small garden accessed through a bright, sunny lounge, and a fence enclosed the rear of the home and on each side to stop residents from wandering off.

Walking to the corner of the front of the "L," Stuart noted the large pool of blood, and slightly behind it towards the front street, there appeared to be a fresh mark gouged or scuffed into the monoblock paving. It was only about an inch long and didn't seem to have a weathered look to it. He glanced behind him and saw that there was a flower bed with the earth piled up against the low wall in a small embankment. The earth was devoid of plants due to the November cold.

For a better effect when the flowers are in bloom, no doubt, he thought before drawing Neilson's attention to it.

"The bullet could be lying in these flower beds, Boss. The search teams better like gardening," he said, knowing that they would have to sieve through all the earth to find it.

"If the round has gone through him, it'll be somewhere around there. It's not like the movies, with bullets bouncing around ricocheting off things. Bullets travel in straight lines," he suggested, having investigated a few shootings over the years.

He also noted several cans and bottles, together with fag ends that had been stubbed out, lying around the flower beds and parking spaces. They would all have to be examined, he knew. They walked around the building as best they could, staying away from the large patch of blood on the monoblock, noting the fenced-off areas to the rear and the railway embankment situated there.

Having satisfied themselves as to the layout of the crime scene, they made their way back to their vehicle, happy that the initial response that had been put in place was what was required to that point. The time was getting on. They both needed a coffee and bacon roll before heading to the post-mortem.

"Might as well head to St Leonards for a quick bite to eat," Neilson suggested, "Its en route anyway," as they walked back to the car.

Fucking ESSO man! Willie thought to himself, smiling inwardly at the derogatory mnemonic used for office-based police -- Every Saturday and Sunday Off – *Needing his tea break already.* But he had to admit, he did feel hungry, and his mouth was dry after last night's beer.

They picked up a takeaway from the station en route to the mortuary in the Cowgate area of the city. The car park was already busy with other vehicles, those also attending the PM – two pathologists who would conduct it, two assistants to help them, along with Neilson and Stuart as SIO (Senior Investigating Officer) and his deputy, staff from the ID Branch, or SOCO, as they would be later known. There was also a couple of DCs who were part of the squad, to take notes. They found a parking space and entered by the side door.

"You ever been to one of these, Boss?" Stuart asked.

"No, I haven't, Willie."

"Can I suggest that you might want to stay back a little? It's pretty messy and a bit gruesome when they get started."

"I've seen dead bodies before. A couple of drug deaths and a bad VA a few years ago."

"A bad car crash is one thing. This is a bit different, though. They're going to take out every organ, examine it, and weigh it. And I mean every organ. After all, it might not have been a bullet that killed him," referring to Neilson's crass comment earlier in the morning. Neilson either chose to ignore it or the comment went straight over his head.

They walked into the main examination area. It was tiled everywhere with three large sinks over to the left. The roller shutter door, which backed onto a tarmacked parking area where hearses could load the deceased into coffins before taking them for burial or cremation services, was closed. Beside the sinks was a bank of refrigerated racks with large doors giving access to three or four six-foot-long tiers where bodies were kept. The people who were required to be there were all in attendance. Neilson knew several of the faces, as did Stuart, but they were just there to observe and make notes or, in the case of the ID Branch staff, record everything on video tape again.

Matty Buchan was lying naked on his back on the trolley under the bright lights of the examination room. The lead pathologist and his assistant, both leaders in their field at Edinburgh University, were about to start. The body had already been fingerprinted, scrapings from under fingernails, and samples from his footwear had also been taken, as well as swabs from his hands and clothing.

"Let's get started, shall we?" the lead pathologist said, taking a scalpel and electric saw to Matty's skull. Cutting through the skin, his face was peeled downwards and the saw quickly gave them access to Buchan's brain. This was examined and weighed. The entry wound in his torso was examined, measured, and then cut open, where it was further explored and an angle of entry established.

Each of his other organs -- heart, liver, and lungs -- were examined in turn for any damage created. They, too, were weighed. The body was examined from the other side where the exit wound gaped widely under his left shoulder blade. Both pathologists spoke as they worked, recording what they were doing and the findings or opinions that they made.

The smell that was generated was nauseous to most people in the room, but they had all experienced it before and had learned to live with it. Looking at dead bodies was indeed one thing, but moving and handling them was quite another. As a young cop in uniform, Stuart had worked on the Lockerbie enquiry at the start when Pan Am 103 had crashed, scattering bodies over a wide area of the Scottish borders. Some of the bodies had never been identified but all of them had received horrendous injuries.

As with many officers, he could deal with the bodies, but it was the looks on their faces and the smells that stayed with him. He had taken to wearing a small face mask with "Vic" menthol rubbed onto the inside of it. After the dead had been photographed in situ, he and the other lads had had to straighten, or sometimes dig, the bodies out in order to get them into the body bags so that they could be transported to the temporary mortuary in the town.

"Definitely a gunshot wound," the lead pathologist said at the end of the three-hour examination. "We've X-rayed him and should find more details about the angle of entry and some micro-fragments from the bullet. It's a large calibre, though. You'll need to find it and the weapon."

"Thanks very much, Professor," Neilson said at the conclusion. "When will we have your findings?"

"As soon as I get out of these overalls, I'll have the notes typed up. Hopefully, quite soon."

"Can we all get back to Craigmillar, please?" he said, turning to his colleagues. "We need to have a briefing about all the info that we have to-date and where we're going with it. Say, one pm?" Nobody said anything to the contrary.

"Fine," Neilson continued, "one pm, Craigmillar."

Stuart had been convinced that Neilson was going to throw his guts up or pass out, but he hadn't.

Maybe, just maybe, I should give him the benefit of the doubt. Somebody in the organisation thought he was the man for the job. Maybe I'm wrong? he mused, as they drove back to the station. They had chatted about where the enquiry would go. Stuart knew each lead, if there were any, would have to be followed up and these leads would generate even more. Stuart knew that they were in for the long haul and that, after the first forty-eight hours, the most important in any enquiry of this kind, the squad would revert to working dayshift hours, and rest-day working and overtime would come to an end. There wasn't an endless money pit and budgets had to be met regardless.

Neilson was turning over in his mind where and how he would steer the enquiry and the direction he hoped to take it.

Chapter Four

Neilson had delivered what Willie Stuart thought to be quite a good speech to the assembled squad the following day. One phrase had stuck in his mind, though, and it had bothered him. When they had returned after the post-mortem, all of the detective constables and their sergeants had been busy when they reached Craigmillar station, and it wouldn't have been appropriate to bring them back to the office or take them away from their enquiries.

"Best leave it 'til the morning, Boss," Stuart had suggested and Neilson had agreed.

But standing before them now, all could see that he was nervous, and he had made a few notes to guide himself along the way.

"Ladies and gents," he began, before summarising the details that were known to those who had been working on the case the previous day and updating those officers new to the case with relevant information. "Overnight and yesterday, the ID of the deceased has been confirmed, as has the cause of death. A gunshot from a large calibre weapon. There are traces of micro-fragments in the chest cavity, and our ballistic boys will come back to us with an angle for the shooter, where he was shot from, higher or lower, et cetera. There are no powder burns on his clothing, so it was from a distance. How far, we don't know. We need to find the bullet. Hopefully, we'll get it today when the search teams widen the search parameters.

"We need to get cracking with witnesses. Let's visit the ones who thought they heard or saw something again and get statements. CCTV trawls need doing thoroughly. Take anything from nearby and we can look at it later. At least it won't be lost. Same applies to traffic cameras and council CCTV. Let's get a hold of it. ID branch have got a load of stuff to examine and that might take a wee while. They've got fag ends, papers, cans, and bottles to fingerprint and DNA. I think we can get a turnaround on that in six hours?" he said haltingly, as he turned to see Stuart nodding.

"I'm going to look at the resources and form up enquiry teams, production officer, et cetera, along with DI Stuart. We're going to be at this for some time. I've been appointed, not because of my detective abilities, but to steer the enquiry. What I would ask, though, is for your full support. I know that many here have been in the CID for a long time and I'm, well, frankly, new to this. If anyone has an idea, a suggestion, or a suspicion please let me know. We'll have a look at what's being suggested, talk it through, and see where it leads or doesn't, as may be the case. When it's all done and dusted, I don't want anyone to say that they thought it was him when we find him. Is that clear with everyone?"

A few of the old hands glanced at each other, thinking the same thing.

Here he goes again. Using everyone to make himself look good for the bosses.

"I'll leave you with DI Stuart and his capable hands. I've got phone calls to make," he finished off, before leaving the briefing room for his office.

Stuart knew most of the detectives in the office and he knew that they were very capable.

"Let's get to it folks. Let's catch the bad guy. I'm going for a fag and a coffee," he said, noting a few wry smiles as he left the room.

Over the course of the day, the teams of detectives visited the old folk's home, the houses, shops, and factory nearby the locus and obtained statements from those who said they had seen or heard something. Lists of those people living there or working the previous day were obtained, to be cross-referred later and possibly interviewed. A lot of the information was useless and would prove to be so, but every piece of information had to be followed up.

Officers tasked with obtaining CCTV did likewise and took away videotapes from cameras covering the front and back of their properties. They might show something, eventually, when they knew what they were looking for. The ID Branch officers were also busy trying to obtain evidence from the items they had collected and were sifting through them as fast, but as safely, as possible, with strict attention to detail.

Early in the afternoon, the search team recovered the round in a flower bed towards the front of the home, lodged in the cement covering of the wall a few inches below the level of the earth raked up against it. The round was forensically recovered, flattened out, similar in shape to a button mushroom. The enquiry team was updated and the round was sent for examination, and it was around this time that Stuart's phone rang again for the umpteenth time that day.

"DI Stuart," he said in monotone into the mouthpiece, cupping the phone against his shoulder and neck as he tried to carry on typing at the computer.

"Happy as ever, Willie?" a cheery voice said down the line, "It's Davie Leadbetter."

"Bedwetter, you old tart! How you doing?" he said with obvious affection for an old colleague with whom he had worked many years ago in uniform, when Stuart had been his sergeant. Davie Leadbetter had also made DI, and Stuart had been at his promotion "doo," but now worked with the Scottish Crime Squad all over the country rather than just in Edinburgh. Organised crime didn't recognise any boundaries.

"I'm fine, Willie. Busy as ever, just like the old days when we used to go tear arsing around the city locking up the bad guys. Stuck behind a desk a bit more now, of course."

"Aye, I know that feeling well. Sucks, doesn't it?"

"Sure does, but Hey Ho, that's the nature of the beast. I hear you're on the Buchan enquiry?"

"I am, indeed. Early days, though."

"And The Prick is SIO?"

"He is, indeed, yes."

"Hard lines. Watch out for him, Willie. I hear he'll knee-drop anyone who crosses him. Carries a grudge, too, seemingly."

"Aye, I know. I've heard the stories, too."

"Listen, mate. I need to speak to you. Are you free for a pint later tonight? I might have something that'll help you."

"Aye, could do. What time are you free of the desk chains?"

"I finish at five. Home for something to eat, so, say, seven pm?"

"I'll plan to get finished about then. I'll meet you straight from work. In town somewhere?"

"Hmmm, maybe not. Somewhere a bit quieter if that's alright, Willie," Leadbetter suggested.

Stuart could sense his young protégé's discomfort.

Must be something he shouldn't be telling me, he thought to himself. "What about the Stable? We all had many a great night in there."

"Perfect, and they do food. I'll grab a scran with you."

"Sounds like a plan, Davie. See you at seven."

Stuart hung up the phone, having given up on his typing. He gazed off, looking out the window of the office, wondering what information Leadbetter had that couldn't be said on the phone. He knew, of course, the Scottish Crime Squad were detectives of above-average ability and commitment, chosen because of their aptitude in surveillance and criminal knowledge and, not least, the capacity to sit and watch a target for long, long periods of time.

Davie Leadbetter, he knew, was talented but had always appeared on the outstanding paperwork lists when he was a constable in uniform. Not because he couldn't do the work, but because he did so much of it. As his sergeant, Willie had written off a lot of superfluous crap for him and fought his corner at every opportunity, when he fell afoul of a senior officer's wrath. No, "Bedwetter" was one of the good guys.

His mind wandered back to the phrase that Neilson had used earlier.

Here to steer the enquiry. What the fuck did he mean, "steer the enquiry"? Enquiries couldn't be steered. Cops followed. They followed where the evidence pointed, one sign post after another, until a logical conclusion was reached and that was the guilt of the bad guy.

Of course, there had been cases where a culprit had been caught and jailed, but who was suspected of other murders. It had then been necessary to trace his movements and actions backwards in order to place him at the locus of the crime and prove his guilt -- the Robert Black enquiry or The Worlds End enquiry, for example. But the trail of evidence had to be found and followed. It was never steered . . .

Chapter Five

The Stable Bar had originally been an old stately home near Mortonhall in the south side of the city. The land on which it stood had been sold many years before and was now a caravan site and a garden centre. The buildings of the old stately home had been converted to flats or apartments with a pub/bistro off the central quadrangle that still retained the cobblestones of old, but which now held tables and chairs rather than horses and carriages.

Being off the beaten track, it suited the caravaners down to the ground as it was not regarded as a local pub and was never really busy.

On walking in, Stuart spotted Davie Leadbetter standing at the bar.

"Hiya, Willie," he said in the same happy way as he'd done earlier on the phone, and they shook each other by the hand, clamping their left hands to the other's shoulder.

"What you having?"

They ordered a couple of pints, took a table in a corner alcove, and perused the menu whilst they chatted, getting updated with how their respective wives and kids were getting on.

"We've had many good nights in here with the old shift, Davie."

"That we have. Christmas doos, leaving doos, and the odd choir practice, too. Remember back when Peter wanted to do an all-night watch on the campsite for the locals stealing out of the tents. He had night sights, binoculars, and everything organised. And then the alarm clock fell out his rucksack! Jesus, that was funny."

When their food arrived, they both tucked in and ordered another couple of beers and after the waitress had gone, Stuart asked, "So what have you got to tell me that's so hush-hush?"

"Right, then. You know how the bush telegraph works and you know how the Scottish works. So this cannot come back to me. You'll have to do a bit of digging on your own and see what you can find. Did you know that we had a job running on Buchan?"

"Eh, no" Willie replied, somewhat surprised, "How long has it been running?"

"A good few months now. We have a guy from outside the Force area trying to get in tight with Buchan. Or at least he was, until a couple of days ago," Leadbetter said.

"Not before time. Buchan was a shrewd cookie. His house has been done loads of times but nothing was ever found – no drugs, no phones, and no notations. We all know that he's a big target, but we could just never pin anything on him."

"Ah, well, there was a change in plan of attack. We were trying to get close to some of his trusted team -- the guys who bought his drugs -- go with them as they did their deals for Buchan and then, when they were coming back with a stash from down south or wherever, they'd get stopped by a random cop or traffic crew – after we had let them know, of course."

Stuart knew only too well how this system worked, having been a DS in the Drug Squad a good few years previously. When they needed to protect their information or sources, a quick call to a local station would get what was sometimes referred to as a "lucky." There was no luck involved.

Leadbetter continued, "The mule would go to court based on what was found in his car, whether or not he wanted to give up any information. With Buchan's lot, there was little chance that the boy would talk anyway. We knew that from the outset. But the guy would get done with possession, possession with intent to supply, and being concerned in the supply of drugs, and would do his time.

"If we did that with several folk close to Buchan, we could then go after him for being concerned in the supply of drugs simply by his association with them. He wouldn't see it coming, confident that he didn't have anything and we had nothing to go on."

"So you wanted his associates only and then just prove his association with guys who were all locked up for drugs offences?" Stuart repeated.

"Exactly," Leadbetter said, "but we ran into a problem. Intelligence. It just dried up, almost overnight. This was a couple of months back."

"Intelligence about who?" Willie asked.

"Everybody in his team."

"We were getting good stuff through the system -- sightings of them, cars they were using, where they were seen frequenting, and who they were talking to. Sometimes there were names, other times just descriptions. We knew when they were flying out on holiday and where they were going through GMP down south, who monitored all tickets bought online. A few got sent right back from the States because they hadn't mentioned drug convictions on their entry forms for the ESTA visa waiver programme."

"So, do you know how that came about --the intelligence drying up?" Stuart asked.

"We did a bit of digging and had to use some computer whizz-kids with that type of thing --the guys that did all that penetration testing work for the Force computer systems. We thought that someone had hacked into the systems or was diverting the intelligence reports about Buchan and his crew. But that all seems to have checked out okay. However, we stumbled over something …"

He paused to take a gulp of his pint. "The local intelligence lads at divisional station HQs get the intelligence reports first and have a look at them. A raw bit of intel," he continued using the colloquialism, "always goes through them first. They read it, evaluate it, and then sanitise it, making sure that the provenance is accurate; you know? How the submitting officer knows it to be true or who the source is, et cetera.

"Well, a lot of good stuff got binned at the start. Only the Intel officers and the submitting officer knew that it had been reported. And unless you went looking for a specific entry that you knew you had submitted and you couldn't find it…? He allowed himself to trail off, posing the question.

"Well, that's a turn-up for the books, Davie. So there's someone on the inside in Buchan's pocket? Hiding stuff that we ought to know about him?"

"I think so, yes. And that brings me to the other thing that I wanted to speak to you about. There's a cop called Hugh Collins. He works in the support unit – does search, public order, and firearms on the ARVs. He was putting in loads of stuff, not just about Buchan and his team, but other stuff, too. He seems to be a well-clued-up dude. It seems that he went looking for an entry that he put in, something that he thought was important, but he couldn't find it on the system. He put it in again and checked for it a few days later, but it still didn't appear."

"How do you know this? What was in the entry?" Stuart asked.

"I don't know what was in the entry, but he kicked up fuck, as you would expect. It seems he was told to wind his neck in. We had a quiet word with the Force Professional Standards Unit, the guys who do the integrity tests on suspected bent cops. They were a couple of the boys that we've used before. You know, boys who can keep 'schtum.' Kind of ironic; isn't it?" Leadbetter paused for effect.

"It's the Professional Standards, after all. Anyway, they put in a couple of entries along the same lines and guess what? Their entries went missing too, but they identified the culprits. So the wheels were set in motion to have these local Intel boys moved out of post for a spurious reason – tenure of post, career development, or whatever, and hey, presto! Things started flowing again. So the boy Collins was right."

"So you know that there are two in Buchan's pocket?"

"At least two, yes. But they don't know that they're in a world of shit right now, and I can't tell you who they are. Like I said before, if it affects your enquiry, you'll have to do the spade work on your own."

"Who did Collins kick up fuck with? Can you tell me that?"

"Professional Standards!" Leadbetter replied.

"So who was in charge of them when this was going on?"

"Take a wild guess?"

"Aw, for fuck's sake," Stuart almost shouted it out, realising where the conversation was going.

"Exactly, Willie, exactly. That's what I said to you on the phone. I think Dick Neilson could be involved. He was the man in charge. I'm assuming that they talk to each other regarding what they're doing and how they're going to do their enquiries. Not to people outside of course, but amongst themselves."

"You'd think so, right?" Stuart agreed. "Do you know who Collins spoke to when he called them about the missing entries?"

"Nope. No idea"

"What about Collins himself? Has he been spoken to?"

"Not by me or any of us. If we did that, we would be letting the cat out the bag about our ongoing job and the two Intel boys that are in the shite. They'll go for neglect of duty at the very least and, more likely, attempting to pervert the course of justice. Plus, we would be opening a huge can of worms. That can wait, as it's got sod all to do with your enquiry, and it's going to have to be done by an outside Force, at a level way above me or you," Leadbetter suggested.

"So Dick Neilson was a CI in Professional Standards and has just come into the CID after submitting a transfer request. He's universally loathed, uses people for his own ends, and fixes cops under him for any mistakes they make, however small, and he's now in charge of the murder enquiry of the man that he could be protecting. He's never done anything like this before, doesn't really know what he's doing, but has a good, experienced team to do the work for him?" Stuart said, summing up the situation for himself.

"And you're his deputy, Willie. For Christ's sake watch your back, mate. There's something going on. What that is and how high it goes, I don't know."

"Right, then. I need to find out who told Collins to wind his neck in, and how they did it – by email or on the phone; why he was told to wind his neck in; what was in the intelligence reports that were submitted but didn't go anywhere; who transferred or appointed Neilson to the murder squad. Oh, and solve the fucking murder, too! And do it all without anyone finding out. Why don't they stick a brush up my arse so that I can do the floor while I'm at it?"

"To a detective of your abilities, Willie, it's a piece of piss," Leadbetter grinned. "How is the enquiry going, anyway?"

"Early days. We've been out getting the statements from those who thought they saw something or heard something; CCTV gathering has been done; we found the bullet that killed him earlier on today. ID Branch will be getting back to us with their results. Neilson's been in his office mostly, allegedly making up the teams and phoning people. I don't suppose you had anyone watching Buchan when he got shot, did you?"

"I wish it were that easy, Willie, and I could give you a witness -- a good witness -- right now. But our boy's been off the grid for a wee while. I'll check when he gets back in touch and let you know if there's anything. Don't hold your breath, though."

"Yes, I know, I know. Listen, though. Thanks for the information, Davie. I'm long enough in the tooth not to make waves for you and I appreciate your going out on a limb for me."

"No worries, Willie. You got me out of a lot of shite in the past. I'm just returning the favour and trying to stop you from getting into it to begin with."

Chapter Six

Hugh Collins returned to work after a day off. Technically, it was two days but he had been in his bed for half of one of them and he was still feeling the effects of his night shifts. Most cops enjoyed the night shift but not starting and finishing them. He and Jamie Beattie had been stood down around five am on the day immediately following the murder, and they had driven back to HQ after unloading their weapons and putting them back into the safe. They sat around the station with coffees waiting on the day shift to arrive before heading home.

As was his normal practise, Collins had had a can of beer before going to his bed without going to the toilet before doing so. He knew that he would be forced to get up early, a full bladder preventing him from just rolling over and going back to sleep. Today, though, he was taking an officer safety class at HQ, a refresher training session for officers regarding holds, use of batons and handcuffs, CS spray, and giving an awareness of other tactics available to them.

At lunch time, he went to his administration department to double-check the shifts he was due to undertake. With the skills that he had, he had to make sure he would be in the right place and carrying the correct gear. He was told that there were to be drugs searches being done over the next two days, and he would be part of an entry and search team.

"Seems the murder squad have made a few phone calls to the drug squad upstairs, asking if they had any live warrants for Buchan and his opposition in the drug trade. They have, and the warrants are going to be executed over the next couple of days," Karen, one of the assistants told him. Collins knew that a drug warrant was valid for a month after it had been issued but also knew that if the intelligence that the drug squad had was any good, they would have hit the house already.

"Sounds like a fishing trip to me," Collins said to her. "The murder squad will be looking for some leads for their enquiry more than recovering drugs. But this'll give them a perfect excuse to search houses and hopefully move things along for them. What time do I parade?"

"Five am, downstairs in the canteen," came the reply.

Jesus, he thought. *Just off the night shift, jetlagged to buggery -- or rather my circadian rhythms were out of alignment –*

wankers speak for jetlag, a phrase that always made him smile, *and now another earlier start.*

He finished the class early, giving the cops the bonus of a flier in return for their hard work and attention during the day. It had been a good class with street cops, well-versed in what they were doing. It was usually a different case with office-based cops and some CID officers, who never used their skills or equipment and who, as a result, had forgotten most of it. Some officers had even attended with their kit still in the box or plastic covering. But because they could be returned to street duties at short notice, they had to have the authorisation to be safe on the street and use the equipment as it was intended to be used.

The following morning, he arrived at HQ at the appointed hour and went to the canteen after picking up his public order bag and search gear. On arrival he met up with several guys from the support unit as well as cops brought in from the divisions who were trained in similar skills. He changed into his public order kit – leg and arm guards, together with his stab-resistant body armour – over which went the flame-retardant overalls and helmet with full-face visor. He then went for a cup of coffee, the makings of which had been provided.

A short time later, the DI from the drug squad arrived and gave a general briefing and provided lists of houses that were to be visited by teams of eight officers -- three in the early morning and possibly a further three later in the day.

At the conclusion of the briefing, they all separated into their respective teams, chatting amongst themselves about who would do what; with the DCs, who would be responsible for anything the teams found and the subsequent enquires that would have to be done. The lead DC, John Reynolds, had the intelligence package -- a plastic folder with the actual warrant to force entry and search the house, signed by the sheriff, together with a diagram of the lay-out of the house so that the entry officers knew in advance where bedrooms would be, as, at this time of day, the occupants were more than likely still asleep.

These layouts were almost always completed and retained for future use. The intelligence pack also had information on the makeup of the front door – wood with wooden surround, one Yale lock, or UPVC with multilock at five points, et cetera. This was important as entry had to be affected quickly to prevent any drugs within the house being disposed of. Most of the officers were well-versed in what was going to happen, and they were soon all in their vans and heading towards their delegated houses. In Collins' case, it was to Gracemount, a first-floor flat of Ryan Docherty, a lieutenant of Buchan.

Collins knew the area well, having worked there a few years previously. Stopping short of the house, the team alighted and followed the team of DCs to the common stair door. While two DCs went to the rear of the premises, the other two lead the team to Docherty's front door and physically pointed straight at it without saying a word, and then they stood back.

The entry team of Collins and Jamie Beattie formed up on the door, one with a "Hooligan" bar, the other with a single enforcer. The "hooli" bar was made from heavy steel, about two feet long, with a large fork at one end designed for ripping off hinges. The opposite end had a duck bill, a two-inch broad curved-steel wedge, tapered to a thin edge with a spike placed at right angles to it. Placing the duck bill against the door, two inches above the lock, Collins slid it along up against the door surround and waited. He looked at the DC who checked his watch and then nodded.

Beattie then used the enforcer, a fifteen kilogram solid metal cylinder with handles on top and at the rear to hammer the duck bill of the "hooli" bar into the wooden surround of the door. He hit it again to bury it deep into the wood. Collins stepped back and, using his considerable strength, ripped the lock out of the door and kicked it open.

Stepping to one side, the remaining teams ran past them quickly in pairs, moving to their allotted rooms, bedrooms first, then lounge, kitchen, and bathroom.

Docherty had been fast asleep when the first officers burst into his bedroom. He was unceremoniously hauled from his bed and placed in handcuffs.

The officers searched the house for other occupants but soon established that he was alone. On the house being declared clear, the DCs entered and explained why they were there and showed him their authorisation to be there.

"Are there any drugs in the house, Ryan?" a DC asked him. "We're going to search the house, anyway."

"If you're going to search the house anyway, why are you fucking asking?" He replied, deadpan. He knew the routine well.

"Just courtesy, and it would save us time and you possible damage to the house."

"Fill your boots then, boys. I'm not saying anything." Docherty had been there before many times and knew the game well.

The entry teams changed into their search boiler suits in the common stair and returned the heavy equipment to the vans, whilst their sergeant sketched the layout of the house again before allocating each of the four pairs of officers a room to search. Collins and his partner Jamie had drawn the living room.

Closing the door behind them, they began to search the room, slowly and methodically, clearing space as they went, always in pairs, for corroboration purposes.

"There's roaches, and plenty of them, in the ashtray," Collins said to his partner as they looked at the coffee table, "along with a hash pipe, bong, and a small stash of 'rat shit.' We'll put everything on the table and sort the notebooks out before we go," he suggested. He didn't get any reply, just a nod from Beattie.

After about seventy minutes, they had just about completed the search. They were on their knees under the window, feeling for any loose wallpaper under the sill, when Collins looked down at the carpet. It wasn't tucked into the gripper rods. He looked to his side and behind him and saw that the carpet was tucked in all around the room. Pulling the carpet back, he saw that the floor boards had been sawn through and a small six-inch square of block board put back in its place with hinges attached to one side. He opened it up and looked in, shining his torch to see.

"What have we, here?" he said, before pulling out a small plastic bag with a small notebook and a SIM card for a mobile phone. Flicking through it with his gloved hands, he saw that it was half-filled with several series of dots and dashes separated by forward slashes.

"That's fucking Morse code!" Collins said in disbelief. "He's using fucking Morse code"

Flicking to the last page, he saw the following:

-../../-.-./-.-//-././-.-./.-../.../---/-.   ...../-----/-----/-----

The date was printed at the far end of each line. Collins was struck dumb.

"What is it, Shug?" Beattie asked.

"Have you got your phone on you? With an internet connection?"

"Aye, I do. Hang on a minute. I'll see if I can get a signal."

"Dial up Morse Code on the internet and see if we can make this out."

For the next several minutes, they plumbed in the series of dots and dashes for the last entry and then both sat back, their mouths agape.

"Fuck me. This is serious!" Jamie said after a few minutes.

"Better get the productions guy in here. Keep it quiet, though."

Jamie went to the lounge door and looked to see first where Docherty was in the house and then where the productions officer was, the guy in charge of logging everything found.

"John," he almost whispered, "come here."

"Aye, what is it?" Reynolds responded rather loudly, but then saw Beattie had his finger up to his lips, shushing him.

"Aye, what you got?" he repeated in quieter tones.

"In here," he said, as they closed the lounge door behind them. "This is absolute dynamite, John." Collins said, before showing him the notebook.

Each officer was wearing latex gloves so as not to contaminate any evidence with their fingerprints. Collins opened the book to show him the series of dots and dashes.

"And your point is?" Reynolds asked.

"I was in the navy cadets back in the day and we did a bit of Morse code back then. I don't think they teach it anymore, but my old man was a radio operator during the war. You know, for flashing messages at sea and stuff like that. I learned a bit from him, too. This is Morse code. We've just sat and Googled it. It looks like it's full of names, numbers next to the names, with dates at the far end."

"Excellent," Reynolds said. "I'll get it logged."

"I don't think you want to do that, Johnny. This has to be kept super-secret right now. The last name is Dick Neilson. Then 5000."

"Fuck me!" Reynolds said.

"Aye, that's what we just said. Why does Neilson's name appear in a drug dealer's notebook, found under the floorboards, with 5000, presumably pounds, next to it? This can't go in through normal channels. You know how these things get out."

"I do, yes. But that's assuming it's our Dick Neilson," Reynolds agreed. "I can't think of any others in the drugs trade right now. Do you know anyone by that name? I think we need to make a phone call. Get a boss in here with enough savvy to know the best way to go."

"I can't think of anyone else, but who are we going to call? Not Professional Standards. I don't trust them. I've had a couple of bad experiences with them already. It can't go back through your guys either, I would suggest." Collins said.

"You're right. It would go through the normal channels and everyone would have access to the information."

"The DI who did the briefing this morning, is this his operation? Was it planned all along or is it a spur-of-the-moment type of thing?"

"Well, between you, Jamie, and me," Reynolds replied, "it's a favour to the murder squad looking into Buchan's shooting the other day. I don't think they have very much to go on right now, and they were hoping that we would turn up something."

"Aye, like the weapon used and a signed confession? But Docherty works for Buchan, or did."

"Yeah, I know. Politics, I think, Shug," Reynolds replied. "Public reassurance that we're on top of the drugs trade; that we're actively seeking the killer and probably to muddy the water by hitting everyone, rather than just Buchan's opposition. After all, it might be someone on his side that's done him in, wanting to be the top dog."

"Do you know who made the phone call asking for the hits to be done?"

"It was the deputy on the murder squad -- a bloke called Willie Stuart. A good guy, apparently."

"Right, then. What about giving him a call and asking him to come here or meet us back at HQ. I'll keep the notebook and we can all make a notebook entry to at least cover ourselves for today. We can see what Willie Stuart wants to do," Collins suggested.

"I'll go with that. What if Docherty wants the notebook back?"

"Well, I don't think he'll broadcast losing it. He's maybe dropped a lot of people in the shite. Right now, we don't know who or how many. Besides, he'll be getting locked up, right?"

"I think we could manage that. We've found enough to show that he's still mixed up in the trade and, with his pre-cons, he'll be expecting it, anyway."

"What's the Morse Code connection all about?" Collins asked innocently.

"Oh, that's easy. Docherty got horsed out the navy after being caught supplying funny fags to his shipmates," Reynolds replied in a matter-of-fact way.

Reynolds phoned the murder squad on his company mobile phone and asked to be put through to Willie Stuart.

"DI Stuart, how can I help you?" he answered.

"Hi, Boss. John Reynolds here from the drug squad. I'm out on the hits with the drug squad this morning. I've got something that will be of interest to you."

"Oh, what's that?"

"I know it's still early in the day and you're up to your arse in work, but could you meet me?"

Christ Almighty, Stuart thought. *Another one of those phone calls where people don't want to say what they've got to tell me,* and then, into the phone, said, "I'm heading down to HQ later in the morning, in about an hour or so. I've got to see how the Ident boys are getting on. Can I meet you there?"

"That would be fine, Willie. It's pretty important and I wouldn't mention it to anyone, you know, that you're going to meet up with us."

The "us" part threw Stuart. He thought back to his phone call from Davie Leadbetter.

"No worries, John. I'll see you in an hour."

"Cheers, Willie."

Reynolds hung up and turned to Collins.

"Right, that's sorted. What to do now, though. The search will be going on for a wee while yet, but Docherty will have to go to the station for an interview, so maybe you could get a lift with the guys taking him?"

"Sounds like a plan. I'll speak to the search team sergeant and make some excuses, and we'll get going. How about Docherty is violent and you feel that you need an OST instructor to help transport him, for health and safety reasons?" Collins suggested.

"I like the way you're thinking, Shug," Reynolds said, and, after a brief conversation, all was in place. The search would carry on, one man short, but that wasn't a problem to the officers who remained. Collins took a bag and placed the notebook and SIM card inside it. He picked up another pair of latex gloves, stuffing them into his trouser pocket. Docherty was escorted from his house and, after dropping him and the detaining officers off at the cells complex, Collins managed to get a lift back to HQ. He grabbed a bacon roll and a coffee at the canteen before going up to the ID Branch offices on the top floor.

"I'm looking for a DI Stuart," he said to the first person he saw sitting at a desk, opposite the open door.

"We don't have a DI Stuart here, mate. This is the ID Branch, are you in the right place?" came the reply.

"He's meeting someone here regarding the Buchan murder enquiry."

"Oh, yeah. That DI Stuart. Yes, he's through at ballistics, next door down," he said, pointing his finger towards the right.

"Cheers," Collins said as he went to find him.

Knocking at the closed door, he didn't stand on ceremony, but entered. Two men were there. "Apologies, gents. I'm looking for DI Stuart," he said.

"That'll be me," Stuart replied, looking up to see Collins' barrel chest and shock of black hair.

"Great. I believe that you were speaking to the drug squad this morning about the hit on Ryan Docherty's house?"

"That's right. What can I do for you?"

Sensing the unease between both parties, the ballistics expert, Peter Watson, said, "Willie, I've still got stuff to do with this bullet. Could you give me thirty or forty-five minutes, and I'll be ready to answer your question?"

Collins and Willie Stuart left the office and walked along the corridor towards the lift.

"I've got some things to say, but we need to be on our own. I work here, so a lot of folks know me. A lot of folks will know you, too. Is there somewhere we could go?" Collins asked.

"There's interview rooms down at the licensing," Stuart suggested, and they headed there in silence, each wondering what the other was thinking about.

The licensing department on the ground floor, where firearms holders, publicans, and foreigners living in the country could all be spoken to and issued their respective authorities, was not busy. Entering one of the interview rooms, they took a seat and talked. After being told what had happened that morning, Stuart sat back in his chair and said, "Fuck me!"

"That's what we all said when we found it," Collins said, almost laughing. "The notebook will obviously have to be translated, decoded, or whatever, to find out what's all in it, but I don't trust anyone here with the information. I don't know how big an issue it is or how high up it goes, and I don't want to get into the shit if anyone finds out that we've got it."

"This is really scary, 'cause I was having almost the same conversation last night with someone else and your name came up, believe it or not. It's cards-on-the-table time, I think," Stuart said, and then told Collins about his conversation with Davie Leadbetter but without mentioning him by name.

"Jesus H Christ," Collins said, letting out a long breath. "Where do we go from here?"

"Where, indeed?" Willie responded. He thought for a few minutes, running various options and permutations through his mind.

"Right, then," he said a long last. "Here's what we're going to do. You keep the book safe. Don't mention to anyone that you've got it. You can't use any Force computers to try to decode it, as someone, somewhere will know you've been logged into the systems, if they go looking. Decode it at home and get as much information from it as you can. If you get into bother with bosses, say I told you to do it this way and for very obvious reasons. I'm going to have to make some covert enquiries into Neilson's background -- where he's worked, who he's worked with, who's got his back, that type of thing, and it's going to take some time."

"Well, I can give you a starter for ten. We were on the same shift for two years, and you'll not find a more back-stabbing, self-centred, conceited wanker in the service," Collins said with obvious venom.

"Well" he chuckled, "don't sit on the fence. Tell me what you really think about him, but at another time and place."

Chapter Seven

Stuart returned to the ID Branch at the appointed time and was updated on the examination of the bullet.

"It's a .308 or 7.62 millimetre round and weighs 150 grains, so it's from a hunting rifle. Unfortunately for you, a 7.62 millimetre round is probably the world's most popular round for hunting rifles," Peter Watson told him.

"Okay. The number of grains matter?" Stuart asked.

"Well, without getting all technical, the more grains in a round, the heavier the bullet; the more it will drop over distance. A lighter round will drop less, but it'll be more susceptible to wind conditions, et cetera. A heavier round wouldn't drift in the wind as much."

"So this is someone who's put a bit of thought into what he's going to do? He's taken the shot from a distance, I think we can agree on that," Stuart suggested.

"Oh, yes, indeed. If Buchan was shot up-close with this type of round, it would've lodged in a wall or something, no problem. Probably would've taken a chunk out of the brickwork, too. These types of rifles shoot at something like 3000 feet-per-second and slow down depending how far the shooter was from his target. This round still had enough energy to go through Buchan and hit a bank of earth and get stuck in a wall. The dirt had slowed it down a good bit, of course. We've got photos of the striations – the rifling -- on the round. All you have to do now is find the rifle that fired it, and, of course, who took the shot."

"What are these rounds used for, then?" Stuart enquired of Watson's superior knowledge.

"Big game. It'll take down deer, antelope, bears, no problem. And, of course, the military uses them."

"Oh, Christ. I hadn't really given that much thought."

"Well, the British Army uses the SA80 and that fires a 5.56 millimetre round. It's not from one of them. A Kalashnikov uses a 7.62, though."

"A Kalashnikov?" Stuart said, almost in disbelief.

"Yes, unfortunately. There's a lot of them down south in the gangland shootings in Manchester, London, and such like. A lot were also brought back by squaddies after the Gulf War; you know? Trophies of war and all that …"

"This'll be like searching for a needle in a haystack of needles, then?"

"Pretty much. But, hey, for a man of your abilities, no problem."

You're the second person to tell me that, Stuart thought.

On the drive back to the murder squad, Stuart had a lot to think about. It had been four days since the murder, and there weren't any definite leads to be followed. The teams of detectives had gathered a lot of information from possible witnesses, and they were being read and re-read by staff, plumbing relevant information into the HOLMES computer system.

The Home Office Large/Major Enquiry System was being fed with key points in order that they could be cross-referenced and nothing would be missed. It had been created to replace a manual card index system that had been used for many years, but it wasn't error-proof. If a witness had made reference to a red car, then both red and car were key points, and anyone referring to either in their statements would be known instantly at the press of a computer key. The system also generated enquiries or tasks that should be followed up.

Information from the ID Branch was now coming in with details of fingerprints identified on cans or bottles found in the car park, or DNA hits from discarded cigarette ends. Each and every one of the identified people would have to be visited, and the reason why they were at the home explained to the satisfaction of the squad.

Then there were the CCTV videos that had to be viewed, recent intelligence had to be scanned, and informers on the streets had been asked to keep their eyes and ears open. Now that they knew what type of weapon had been used for sure, a trawl through the registered firearms certificate holders would have to be completed. Stuart suspected that that was unlikely to turn up the weapon, but not impossible. It was more likely to have been an illegally held weapon and he knew a national enquiry would have to be undertaken to see if other crimes had been committed using the same type of weapon, or if any such weapon had been stolen recently, or indeed, long ago. Then his mind switched to Neilson. What about him? He hadn't covered himself in glory to-date.

He'd tried to busy himself with ordering stationery, organising staff, and double-checking everything that the team had done so far. He hadn't lead the enquiry at all; if anything, he was playing catch-up or treading water, trying to give the impression that he knew what he was doing. In reality, he was out of his depth and the team knew it, judging by the sometimes stupid questions he had asked.

Stuart had heard the story about Neilson when a surveillance team had been watching a member of Buchan's opposition and their car had been spotted, or "burnt," in common parlance. "Have the insurance forms been completed?" he had enquired to the amusement of all present. But was he involved in corruption? Was he the Dick Neilson in the notebook? If he was, how far back did it go and how much was involved? What was the connection with Buchan? Who else was involved?

It's enough to give your arse a sore head, he said to himself as he pulled into the station.

"I've got the results of the ballistics, Boss," he said to Neilson. "Just a verbal right now, the paperwork will be coming," he said, before explaining what he had been told earlier.

"Hmm," Neilson mused. "We need to find the weapon, Willie."

"We do, yes," he agreed, before outlining where he felt the thrust of the enquiry should go.

"What about the local enquiries first, though?" Neilson questioned.

"Well, that can still go on. The guys at firearms licensing could look through their database for .308 or 7.62 millimetres, and enquiries at a national level will be done by other forces, anyway. We'll have to look at getting the army involved to see if they have had any misuse of their weapons, or if they know about any squaddies with war trophies. That's going to be difficult."

"Ah, yes, yes, that's a good idea. Thanks, Willie. I'll organise that," he replied, before disappearing back into his office again.

He'll be away to phone the bosses upstairs with an update on how he's had a great breakthrough, no doubt, Stuart thought to himself, before going into his office and firing up his computer terminal. He had some enquiries to make, as well as a few phone calls.

Turning to the computer, he logged into the management system containing officers' details. He looked up Neilson and wrote down his personal mobile telephone number and read through the other details that were listed, but it didn't offer much help.

Next, he logged into the training directory which listed courses that officers could take and were designed for self-improvement. Of course, an officer would have to be nominated or apply for some of the courses, but he could see which ones Neilson had undertaken. Pretty much what he expected to find. He did see that Neilson had administrative rights for the intelligence system, which would have allowed him to alter, send back, or delete entries as he saw fit. Any entry so amended would have a time and date stamp on it and who had made the change. That was something he would have to explore further, he knew.

He dialled into the crime computer looking to see if any .308 or 7.62 rifles had been stolen. He started by going back a year, without success, but then found that a Remington rifle had been stolen during a house break at a farm in the town of Lauder, in the Scottish borders country, about eighteen months previously, and one, a Blaser, about two years ago in similar circumstances, from a farm in Hawick.

He printed out copies of the crimes and read through the contents of the listed enquiries that had been done on screen, while the printer churned out the paperwork. Both crimes had been unsolved and, in each case, the firearm had been held appropriately, locked away in a secure cabinet. In the case of the Blaser rifle, however, he saw that a partial fingerprint had been found but remained unidentified. That was something else he would have to explore, he thought, as he retrieved the paper copies of each crime and folded them up, putting them in his jacket pocket.

Picking up the phone, he called the Human Resources Department and spoke to one of the assistants. Identifying himself, he asked her, "Can I access the record of an officer? It's to do with the Buchan murder enquiry. I can't really say much more."

"It's not something that is usually done, Inspector."

"I understand that, but, like I said, it's part of the on-going murder enquiry."

"We like to know in advance who the officer is so that we can look at the file to make sure everything relates to that officer. You know, just in case something has been misfiled."

"Yes, I understand that, too. I can sign an authorisation for you if you want me to." Stuart hated "red tape," and he was being stone-walled with it.

He was getting impatient. He recalled the time when he had submitted a small slab of cannabis, wrapped in cling film, for confirmation of it being a controlled drug. It had been sent back to him with a terse note outlining that he hadn't detailed the type of enquiry he wanted done. Phoning the admin clerk back, he'd apologised and said that he needed it fingerprinted.

"Why?" they'd asked him, "it's hash!"

"Fucking exactly," he'd roared into the phone, before slamming the handset down.

He'd got a proper row for that one, he remembered fondly.

"Well, if it's important, I suppose you could." Stuart asked for her name and said that he would contact her later and make arrangements to come and see her. It was, after all four pm, and she would be going home. Thanking her for her help, he hung up the phone.

Stuart signed off the computer terminal and quickly poked his head into Neilson's office.

"That's me away, Boss. Day off tomorrow." He was telling him, not asking.

Neilson was on the phone and just nodded as Stuart turned and left. He wasn't going home, however. He was going to meet up with Collins at his house to see how he was getting on with the notebook and SIM he had found earlier.

He arrived at Collins' flat in a quiet suburban area and rang the doorbell. Collins answered and ushered him into the living room of the house. Stuart looked at the photos on the wall – a young Mr and Mrs Collins' wedding photograph, no doubt – and could see the place was littered with paper, and a laptop was up and running.

"Been busy, then?" Willie enquired.

"Aye, you could say that," Collins responded. "Found out some good stuff, though, and I've been writing it all down. You want a coffee?"

"Yeah, please. Just milk."

Whilst Collins busied himself in the kitchen, Willie looked through the pages of foolscap. The names were a "who's who" of the drugs trade in Edinburgh, some of whom he recognised from his previous dealings with them.

"There's a few well-known names in here, Shug," he said, after Collins came back with the coffees, "and a few I've never heard of, but somebody will know them."

"Probably, but I don't think that we can go public with any of this stuff until we know what we're dealing with. That'll have to wait."

"Where does Neilson figure in all this?" Stuart asked, sipping his coffee.

"From what I can tell, only recently. Maybe the last eighteen months to two years. It looks like he's getting 5000 pounds per month, which, if these are sums of money and the figures are right, it's pretty much small money in the grand scheme of things. There's about 100 to 150k noted here, just this year."

"Is this money that he's getting, though? It could be how much the names in here owe Buchan, or the amount of drugs that Buchan has got stashed away with them. We'll have to clarify that, somehow."

"You're right about that. There aren't any phone numbers in the notebook that I can see. I was about to have a look at the SIM card when you rang the doorbell."

"Lay on, Macduff," Stuart said, referencing his love of Shakespeare and his often quoted lines.

Collins put on a pair of latex gloves again and took his own mobile phone apart. Removing the SIM card, he inserted the one he had found and turned the phone back on. Moving through the various menus, he quickly found the contacts list.

"You ready for this?"

Stuart picked up a sheet of paper and took out a pen. As Collins reeled off the names and phone numbers, he wrote them down, reading them back to make sure he had heard correctly. Many of the names on their lists from the notebook were in the phone contacts on the SIM card. After several minutes of writing, they reached the end. Neilson's number wasn't listed.

"It was worth a try. I noted his mobile earlier. I didn't think he would be stupid enough to give Buchan his own mobile number," Stuart said. "Don't suppose you know who the service provider is for the SIM, do you?

"I think it's O2, but I'd be very much surprised if there's a contract involved. This'll more than likely be a pay-as-you-go type of phone. Maybe we could contact O2 to see when the SIM free phone was originally sold and to whom? You know, just by them searching on the number?"

"That's possible but would need authorisation from a Super as to why we wanted the information. Data Protection and all that," Stuart reminded him.

They both knew that telephone companies could provide details to police but only as part of an ongoing enquiry, and unauthorised use of information held on computer was a major issue and was rigorously investigated if a breach of protocol was suspected. They sat back and sipped at their coffee, thinking.

"What about Crime Stoppers?" Collins suggested. "What if we made a couple of anonymous phone calls to them with some information in here?"

"Best case scenario would be that the drugs squad would hit the house. They'd maybe find more intelligence and maybe a good recovery of gear, but that's a long shot. We don't have addresses here, anyway. Worst case is that they wouldn't act on it at all."

"Yeah, I suppose you're right there," Collins agreed.

"What if we were to get a hold of Ryan Docherty? If he gets out after Court or even if he gets the jail, we could put him under a bit of pressure. You know, let him know that we know he's dropped a lot of people in the shite. If he doesn't play ball, we would let it slip to certain people who would do him serious damage. He must be shitting bricks right now," Stuart suggested.

"If you think that's the best way to go, then, yes. I'll go along with it."

"Well, he's going to figure in the murder enquiry, anyway. So we could kill two birds with the one stone. I'll make sure I speak to him. Now," Stuart said, changing the subject, "what about Neilson?"

"If this book is right, Neilson first pops up in about April last year. There's an entry for him every month up until now, you know, the last entry I found today. If he's getting 5000 pounds a month, that's a lot. They could be using him to pass it on, right enough, or maybe hide the money for Buchan and his team. But why? Why would he be doing this?"

"Ah, the 64,000-dollar question. Who knows? Greed, coercion, money troubles. He might even be Buchan's pal. Oh, what a tangled web we weave, when we practise to deceive."

"What?" Collins asked, confused.

"Nothing. It's just me," Stuart replied, smiling to himself.

"But, then, you said you worked with Neilson?" Stuart asked.

"I did that. Worked for him, more like. Lazy bastard. Any job we went to, he always played a Mexican standoff with his notebook. You know, he'd hardly ever volunteer to note details of a job. At car crashes, he'd be first out to direct traffic so it looked like he was busy but never had any paperwork to do. Spent all his time studying books. When he did get details of a job, he always had to go straight back to the station to phone it in, like they would somehow disappear." Stuart was nodding his head. He knew exactly the type of officer, having met similar when he had been a shift sergeant.

"He was always slow to help out in a fight or take on protracted enquiries. He'd do the easy stuff or write out tickets, no problem," Collins carried on, "but it became embarrassing. He reached the bottom of the barrel in my book when he charged a bloke for not producing his driving documents within the seven days. He brought them in on the eighth day, all in order, but he still fixed him. Made him look good to the bosses, but the guys on the shift hated his guts.

"He talked a great game and used all the experiences of the shift to pad out his CV and got promoted on the back of it, but he had never done very much of what he said he'd done. He was also a loudmouth when he'd had a few pints, dropping names and bragging about the great arrests that he'd made, when we all knew he'd only been a second witness. It got him into a few tight situations on nights out, where guys from the team wanted to fill him in, let alone Joe Public."

"How was that not picked up on?" Stuart asked.

"You tell me. You've been promoted. I've never played that game. I just want to be the best cop I can be and lock up the bad guys."

Stuart did indeed know how the game was played. It was never about what you had done, it was about how you said what you had done. There were even instances of people being promoted to get them out of the way.

"Anyway," Collins continued, "we had a big falling out. He wouldn't corroborate a drug recovery I had made. Not a big recovery, just personal-use stuff, but he'd been away hobnobbing somewhere instead of doing his job when I found it. Like I had planted it on the guy, or something. This was at the cells. Well, the Inspector tore him a new arsehole. He got sent somewhere else and our paths never crossed until later, when he got promoted to planning department. After that, every detail I got sent on – football, rugby, demos, and marches – I got the shit end of the stick. When he got promoted again, into the complaints, he left no stone unturned in his efforts to get me done with something or another. By Christ, he can carry a grudge. Well, that's what I thought, anyway."

"Have you done anything about it? A grievance?" Stuart asked.

"Tried to," Collins replied, "but every time I tried, I met a brick wall. Last time was the intelligence reports I put in a few months ago. The ones that disappeared. I informed the Professional Standards about it and nothing happened. And you know who was in charge by then? Dick the Prick! Promoted again to Chief Inspector. Call me a cynic, but it looks like you get a Teflon coat at CI level these days. Nothing sticks to you."

"What was in the entry you put in? The one you went looking for?" Stuart asked.

"I'd seen Buchan going into the old folk's home a few times -- the one where he got shot. I made a few enquiries and found out his mother lived there. Buchan visited about the same time every week because of his mum's condition."

"Has he ever succeeded in nailing you, then?"

"Just the once. A couple of years back, I recovered a guy's laptop that had been stolen; did the report and sent the lap top to HQ to be retained for Court; went to Court and it was produced for me and everyone else to identify, as you do. I gave it back to the Court officer and thought nothing else about it. A couple of weeks later, the owner, wanting it back, complained that he couldn't get it. It couldn't be found. I got done with not looking after my productions, despite doing everything that I was supposed to. I got one of those written warning things. The boss who did it was embarrassed to say the least."

"What about the grievance you tried?" Willie asked. "What reason did they give?"

"Clash of personalities. A Clash of fucking personalities!"

"But you'd like to see him hang out to dry?"

"Without a shadow of a doubt. And with extreme prejudice, please," he smirked in response.

"Okay, then, let's see what we can do about that." Stuart then told him about the break-ins to the two houses in the borders, where rifles had been stolen.

"Well, that's my field, if you'll pardon the pun. I know the area. I'm into the shooting and fishing down there and have loads of contacts. I could ask around and see what I can get."

"And I'll lean on Ryan Docherty and hold his feet to the fire."

Chapter Eight

Richard Neilson had indeed gone to school with Matty Buchan, although Willie Stuart and Hugh Collins would not find this out until much later. Neilson was an only child and had been sent to private school, largely on the proceeds of the death benefit and large pension his mother had received after his father had been killed in a car crash. He had done well at school but had problems mixing with his fellow pupils, preferring the company of a small group of friends, something his teachers and mother attributed to his being an only child and to losing his father at an early age.

She doted on her only child, spoiling him at every opportunity, as did his elderly grandparents. He had a few interests outside school -- cross-country running or training in a gym on his own, never in team sports. His passion was the military, particularly the history of weaponry, and he had joined the school cadet force, notwithstanding his awkwardness in large groups, where he had learned weapons-handling drills and the skills involved in shooting.

He worked hard and his grades were good enough to allow him to attend university, if he so wished. It had been in his final year at school when he had got himself into trouble with authority, being caught in the company of a group of boys smoking cannabis on the school grounds. The school had made their own internal enquiries before contacting the police, hoping that they could deal with the matter themselves.

However, the staff had found more drugs in a locker and the owner of the locker had been one of their number, Matty Buchan. Everyone was aware that Buchan had been in trouble countless times before, but this was the last straw, and he had been charged by the police. The remaining boys were used as witnesses against him. As a fifteen-year-old, Buchan couldn't be reported to Court but was dealt with as a child and appeared with his mother before a children's panel. He was, of course, expelled from the school.

In due course, Neilson did go to university to study history, but, disliking certain aspects of the course, dropped out after year two and applied to join the police. His family's friends provided glowing references, of course, and after his initial training, he joined a shift at a local station in Edinburgh, where the rough and tumble nature of police work, the constant change of practices and procedure, the continual demand for his time, and the often harsh banter of his colleagues, was not to his liking.

It had been an astute sergeant who had first noticed and recognised his personality traits and who had sent him to the Force medical officer. It was he who suspected that Neilson had Asperger's Syndrome, which was confirmed by psychological examination and which accounted for his sensitivities, lack of creativity, and dislike of change, amongst others traits. Nevertheless, he again studied hard to pass his police exams, determined to get away from street duties and into the smaller, more intimate surroundings of office work. In this way, his career progressed, eventually being promoted twice more.

It had been one day, during the last few weeks of his time on the streets, when he had met up with Matty Buchan again. Whilst processing a prisoner at the cells complex, Buchan had been brought in, having been fighting outside a pub and resisting arrest, by other officers. They had recognised each other but said nothing, as they both knew that they were being filmed and recorded. However, a month later, Buchan had phoned him.

"Hiya, Rich," he had said in a loud, confident manner.

"Sorry. Who is this?"

"Ah, don't be like that. We were at school together, and we bumped into each other again at St Leonards a wee while back."

Neilson's heart sank. He knew that Buchan was a big player in the drug scene, having been told by his colleague.

"I was wondering if you could do me a favour," Buchan asked.

Neilson knew that he owed him a favour, and they both knew Neilson had been a witness against him. Buchan, he had been told, was not a person to take "no" for an answer, with a hugely volatile temper.

"I didn't realise you'd joined the Force? How long you been doing that?" Buchan continued.

"Yes, about four years now. How are you?" He answered, warily.

"Doing fine. Business is good but it's a competitive market. You know how it is, and there are occupational hazards. Perhaps you could help me with some of them? I know you from way back. I wonder if your bosses know about you helping me out back in the day. After all, the stuff in my locker all those years ago wasn't just mine, was it?"

The implication was obvious, even to Neilson. His mind raced, struggling to come up with a reply that would put an end to the conversation. He knew that the drugs found at school weren't just his. They were Buchan's, too. But he also knew that he would be investigated if any allegations were made. They would find out that he knew Buchan, and his career path could be affected. He had just been promoted, after all. He could change his phone, he knew, but Buchan had found him once already and he could do it again. It was Buchan who closed the conversation.

"I'll be in touch with you. Maybe drop in for a coffee one time?" he said before hanging up.

"Eh, yes, okay" he had replied in a half-hearted manner.

It was only a short time afterwards that Buchan began to make numerous complaint allegations against him – theft of money whilst processing a prisoner, or failing to act on a piece of evidence. Doing so anonymously, at first, he then had his associates do the same, which, although they proved to be unsubstantiated, nevertheless placed Neilson under close scrutiny from the Professional Standards Department.

As a result, he withdrew further into his shell, as his confidence in his position dwindled. Lacking anyone to confide in, he came to believe that he could only help his situation by giving in to Buchan's demands. He knew he was on the hook and, when Buchan called on him outlining what he expected in no uncertain terms, he could only agree.

Neilson would supply Buchan with details of intelligence that the police held on him, give advance warning, when he could, of impending operations against him and details of his opposition. In return, he supplied Neilson with snippets of information that would take out his opposition and which would also curry favour for Neilson in his boss's eyes. As his career progressed, he would still keep access to the information Buchan wanted. Despite him putting in many transfer requests away from the City, Buchan hounded him relentlessly and, as the years went by, Neilson was sucked deeper and deeper into the mire as more information was passed and money changed hands.

Now, thirteen years later, Neilson stared out of his office window, deep in thought, wishing he had told Buchan to fuck off a long ago, and tried to think of where the enquiry into his death would go next and how he could account for his past discretions, should they be divulged. He had, after all, taken his time and thought the matter through; hadn't he?

"Morning, Boss," Stuart said, popping his head around the door and bringing Neilson back to the present.

"Apologies for missing the briefing this morning, but I was otherwise engaged looking at the latest intelligence coming in from the drug squad hits over the last couple of days. Not much, I'm afraid," he lied.

After his day off, which had really been a day off, spent golfing with a few friends despite the winter greens, he had not been thinking about work. He hadn't slept well since the day of the murder, with everything that was going through his head. But now, a week into the enquiry, he felt that his batteries had been recharged and was getting "match fit" again.

Stuart had in fact called into Police HQ that morning and had gone to the HR Department where he had been granted access to Neilson's file. He had thumbed through it, not sure what he was looking for, but stumbled over the letter from the medical officer and psychologist outlining their diagnosis of Neilson's Asperger's and their recommendation that he should be put on office duties. He found letters from referees going back to when he had joined – glowing references, indeed -- with details of his interview and promotion panels, and his one confirmed brush with the complaints department that Collins had already told him about, which had resulted in a "counselling" from a senior officer, or a good old-fashioned row back in the day.

Stuart busied himself about the office and brought himself up to speed with how the enquiry was progressing. After several hours of reading, there was not a lot to report. The DCs were tracing people that needed to be spoken to and had been prioritised by the sergeants after checking with Neilson. He had agreed, of course, but whilst reading through a checklist of items that had been submitted from the ID branch he noticed that Hugh Collins' name appeared on the list. A cigar butt had been recovered at the rear of the old folk's home and his DNA was on it. Collins would have to be spoken to. He sat back in his chair again.

For fucks sake. He can't be involved, can he? he thought, second-guessing his judgment.

He picked up the phone and called the firearms licensing department, where he spoke with an assistant.

"You know how we asked you to give us a list of anyone in the Force area who owns a .308 or 7.62 rifle? Well, could you have a look for a guy called Hugh Collins?"

"We're doing the list right now. There's quite a lot," came the reply, "but hang on a minute."

After several minutes, the voice came back on the line.

"Sorry about that, but I had to go across the room to another terminal. Yes, he's a firearms certificate holder. He has a Blaser .308."

He offered his thanks and hung up. He sat back in his chair again and thought to himself, *The enquiry had been running for about a week now. Actions are being generated thick and fast as more and more information is inputted. It was only a matter of time until Collins' name came up.*

He knew that every police officer's fingerprints and DNA were taken when they joined the Force, but they were only taken for elimination purposes and were kept separate from the main database. They could only be accessed by an application to the Deputy Chief Constable via the head of Professional Standards. Someone must have asked for the cops file to be checked. Why would they do that? Especially this early in the enquiry? Do they know something we don't?

All these questions went through his head but he couldn't reasonably answer any of them.

Double, double toil and trouble; fire burn and cauldron bubble, he thought to himself again, remembering another of his favourite Shakespeare quotations.

"I need a fucking fag," he said to no one. "This gets worse by the day."

Chapter Nine

The Scottish Borders is situated about an hour's drive to the south of Edinburgh and is a hunting, shooting, and fishing hotspot. Beautiful rolling hills and open farmland, made popular by Sir Walter Scott who lived at Abbotsford near the small town of Melrose, were full of game, and the River Tweed, which forms the boundary with England, was usually prolific in terms of salmon numbers caught. The fisherman had to be in the right spot at the right time, of course, but Collins had enjoyed many days fishing the river, with or without catching anything. Huge tracts of land surrounding the area is owned, for the most part, by titled families such as the Duke of Roxburgh or the Duke of Buccleuch, and they ran organised shooting parties on their grounds, overseen by their ghillies and gamekeepers, targeting pheasants, partridges, and deer when in season.

Collins, of course, could not afford to move in such vaulted circles but he was occasionally invited as a guest of a friend who could. His shooting was restricted to vermin control on farmers' lands, targeting mainly foxes, rabbits, and pigeons, but he was a member of a syndicate, a group of like-minded friends, really, who clubbed together, buying young pheasants to rear throughout the year, which they could shoot when they became mature. It could be hard work looking after them, but the cost of the shoot was considerably less onerous on his pocket. Over the years, he had spent a lot of time in the Borders indulging his passion for fishing and shooting, and his shift colleagues had enjoyed his catches of salmon or game pie at refreshment time.

Collins had been busy following his conversation with Willie Stuart. He made a couple of phone calls to friends who lived and worked in the Borders area and, in such a tight, close-knit community, there wasn't a lot that went on that people did not get to hear about. He asked the gamekeepers and ghillies he spoke to if they had heard of any rifles having been stolen in the last couple of years, but none had. They did promise to ask around with their fellow ghillies to see if they knew anything, and they would get back to him.

Having done this, he wrote out a list of the mobile telephone numbers that he had obtained from Docherty's SIM card, before replacing his own SIM card back into his phone. He placed all the documents in a plastic sleeve, keeping the notebook and SIM card separate and preserved as best he could. He had tried to get to sleep after that but passed a fitful, restless night, trying not to disturb his wife too much, before admitting defeat and rising at four am for the second sweep of drugs searches that he was scheduled to undertake. He knew that he would be on three rest days afterwards and that was when he planned to follow up on his enquiries.

He paraded for duty at five am as he had done before, and he was approached by John Reynolds. "How'd it go yesterday? Did you meet up with Willie?" he asked.

"I did, yes. I think we've got all the information that we can from the notebook, but it's opening a big can of worms. This has to stay on the quiet, John. Nobody can find out we've got it."

"Yeah, I know, I know."

"Was Docherty locked up yesterday?"

"He was, yes. It wasn't a big recovery against him but enough to keep him. Part of the grand scheme of things. You know the drugs operation. I think he'll get out at Court today, though."

"Not enough to remand him, then?"

"No, not really. He'll be back out later today."

As it turned out, there was only one series of houses that were to be raided that morning and all the uniform staff were overjoyed when they were told that it would be "job and finish" – they would not have to return to their normal duties afterwards. The CID officers would have to complete all their enquiries, however. The raids went smoothly with nothing much gained in return for their collective efforts, and Collins had gone home around midday to enjoy his time off.

It was a couple of days later when he took a call from one of his ghillie friends, telling him about the break-in to the farmhouse in Hawick.

"Seems Harry wasn't quite as truthful with your colleagues as he could have been," the ghillie said to him.

"Who's Harry?" he asked, confused.

"Harry King's quite a well-to-do farmer down here; owns lots of land and does a lot of shooting, but he's got a drink problem. Well, he's an alky, if truth be told. Turns up pished to go shooting or gets pished at the shoot. That's bad enough when he's driving or fishing, but where guns are concerned …" He trailed off.

"You're right, there. Guns and booze shouldn't mix," Collins agreed.

"Anyway, because of that, he's not very popular. It seems he got taken home this day, after the shoot. He was almost paralytic. It was the following day that he called you guys to say that his house had been broken into and his rifle and ammo stolen."

"So his house wasn't broken into?" Collins asked, wondering why he'd used the phrase, "*said* his house was broken into."

"I don't know; neither does Harry. He was so pished he can't remember. He woke up in the morning to find a window smashed and his rifle cabinet open. It was good gear, too, by all accounts."

"Do you know who took him home?"

"Sorry, I don't. But you know that if the police got to find out that he was unsafe to be a firearms holder because of his drinking, they'd take the guns off him in a heartbeat."

"Absolutely," Collins agreed.

"But, then, the estate will have details of who was there and what was shot. Why don't you ask there?" the ghillies suggested. "Is this a big case you're on? I would've thought that the local boys down here would be doing it."

"Yeah, I know, but it's just something that we stumbled over up here, and we need to get to the bottom of it. Thanks for your help on this," Collins said before hanging up.

No time like the present, he thought, and besides, he liked the Borders and it was a nice day for a drive. He jumped in his car and drove southwards through the various little towns and villages that were dotted here and there, over the river Tweed where the Ettrick tributary joined it, and where he stopped to watch a couple of fishermen for a few minutes as he smoked a cigar.

He found the Buccleuch Estate offices without much trouble. Driving in past the lodge house at the entrance to the estate, he made his way along the road, passing the manicured gardens to the estate offices. Next to the mansion was the "big hoose," where the landowner lived when not sitting in the House of Lords in London.

He introduced himself, explaining that he was interested in one or two day's deer stalking, if they had any availability and, of course, what the cost would be.

"The factor of the estate is not available right now, but perhaps I can answer your questions?" a nice looking young lady suggested to him.

Collins explained that he did a little shooting and wanted to shoot a sika stag, a close relative of the famous red deer. Might he have a look at the game register to see when the best time would be to book?

"Of course. Just follow me," she said, and they walked to an adjoining office where the walls were lined with books. She handed him the previous two years' registers of deer that had been shot. As with all things, records had to be kept in order that the estate would remain profitable and that they maintained a good stock of animals for their clients.

To that end, the game register was kept with dates, type of animal taken -- sika or roe deer -- whether it was a stag or a hind (stags being more expensive), its weight, and details of who had shot it.

"These records are very well kept," Collins said to her.

"We try to run a tight ship here, and I think that we offer good value for money."

"Yes, I'm just looking through the various months. I see September and October seem to be the best months, even going back a couple of years," he said, as he continued to leaf through the book. "Are guests details noted here too or just the tenants?"

"If someone has shot a beast, their name will be in here. I'll leave you to it just now. I shouldn't leave the office."

Collins had gone back several months but still hadn't found what he was looking for. But then he found it.

September 13th two years before. Mr R Neilson. 150lb hind, guest of Mr H King.

The day before Harry King's house had been screwed.

He sat back in his chair and quickly took out his mobile phone. Turning on the camera he took a couple photographs of the page and put his phone back in his pocket. He then walked back into the office and asked for contact details for the estates office and said that he would be in touch shortly to try to organise his day. Climbing back into his car, he thought about phoning Willie Stuart to update him, but he couldn't get a signal. *Yes,* he thought, *the Borders are great but the phone coverage is crap.*

On the drive back to the main road, he thought about what he should do. He couldn't just phone the local officers and ask them to open the enquiry again. After all, it had been over two years before and it would mean giving them access to the information that he and Willie had gathered. Hawick wasn't too far from the estates offices and he thought about calling in to see Harry King, but decided against it. Best do it when he was on duty. But how could he be on duty in Hawick; he worked in Edinburgh. Maybe best to check the firearms register when he was next on duty to see if Harry King was still a certificate holder.

Fuck it, he said to himself, *I'm days off and need a few pints,* and put the thoughts he had out of his mind as best he could on the drive back to Edinburgh.

After all, we're holding all the aces right now and very few people know that we've got a good hand. There was him, Willie, John Reynolds, and, of course, Jamie Beattie who had been there when I found the notebook. He stopped himself in mid-thought.

"Jesus. You're doing it again. Give it a rest. I'll phone Willie when I get back on duty and that's that," he said out loud.

Chapter Ten

Collins had indeed gone out for a few pints when he got back home. Leaving his car at home, he walked to his local rugby club and watched the tail end of the game that was going on. He had played there many years before with many of them, still knew a lot of the old faces and with whom he had had many a great day and night. And that's exactly how this day had panned out. The afternoon turned into an evening, and then into a late night, with the beers flowing and tales of daring-do regaled for the umpteenth time.

It had been through rugby that he first realised how much he enjoyed the Borders area, a hotbed of rugby. The towns of Galashiels, Hawick, Kelso, Selkirk, or Melrose each had a wonderful sense of community spirit and enjoyed a fierce rivalry on and off the rugby pitch. These towns each had several rugby teams and such was the pride that the town took in their rugby that members of the public would stop players in the street after a game, offering advice on how a player could improve or what they had done well. It was all about bragging rights until the next time they played.

He had enjoyed his time off and felt refreshed when he came on duty for a backshift the following Monday. After he and his partner, Jamie, had been brought up-to-date with the events of the weekend generally, they had been given their warning as before by their Inspector Willie Dunn and had gone out on patrol. Without any specific tasking of their firearms talents, they drove around Edinburgh, tuning into the radio channels as they went from area to area listening out for any jobs that they could assist with, such as raid alarms at shops or backing up their uniform colleagues, if they were nearby.

It was around six-thirty that evening when the vehicle mobile phone rang. Somebody had changed the ringtone to Darth Vader's March from Star Wars, which made them both smile.

"Hello. Alpha Victor 1. Shug Collins speaking," he said into the handset.

"Shug, it's Willie Dunn. Get over to Cameron Toll. Someone's pistol whipped a guy in the grounds of Liberton Rugby Club and made off after the training lights were turned on. The culprit has made off towards the Inch Park. As of now, you're authorised to go red."

The Inspector then passed the details of the officer on the scene at the locus and the radio channel on which to contact him.

"Okay, Inspector. We're west side right now, but we'll get onto the bypass and should be there pretty quick."

Collins turned to Jamie and said, "We're red. A job over at Cameron Toll. Find a place to park up, mate."

Jamie drove into a side street and parked the vehicle. They both got out and went to the rear of the hatchback car and opened it up. Jamie unlocked the top drawer of the safe and they delved in, each taking out an H & K G36 and a magazine. Slotting it into place, they drew back the working parts and let them slide forward on the spring, loading the weapon. The G36 was slung around their body with a retaining strap.

They each took an H & K Glock 19 pistol, repeating the action and placing the weapons in the holsters they were already wearing. Jumping back into the vehicle, Jamie drove off with Collins, activating the flashing lights and two tones. He then turned to the folder within the glove compartment and began writing notes with the information that had been passed to him. There was always paperwork to do, and it was best that they made notes as they went.

They were not long in arriving at the rendezvous point near to where the incident had happened. They spoke with the officers who had stumbled over the incident. The local sergeant and inspector had already attended to keep an oversight on the events.

"Who are we looking for?" Collins asked.

"A young male, maybe twenty-four or twenty-five. Dark green jacket, dark trousers. About six feet tall, with blond hair, cut short."

"Where did he go?"

"I think he headed in the direction of the back of the shopping centre. You know where the rugby pitches are?"

Collins did indeed know, having played there many years before and where he had first experienced the excruciating pain of a "stinger" in his neck.

"And what type of weapon?"

"Small handgun type of thing, definitely not a long barrel. It was being pointed at the complainer with the guy standing over him, when the informant snapped on the training lights."

"No need for plates, then, Jamie," he said to his partner. A rifle would require them to wear ceramic plates in their body armour, a significant additional weight they both could do without. Then to the local Inspector and sergeant he said, "Can we put a box on the outside of the park on the road? If he leaves, get your boys to give us a shout. Is there a dog en route?"

"Dog handler has been requested and is attending, as far as I know," the inspector replied.

"Are you happy with that, then, Boss?"

"Fine by me," came the reply.

Jamie and Collins were then off and running – jogging, really, with the weight of equipment and weapons they were carrying – and they made their way into the darkness of the park, totally unaware of the direction the male had made off in. The only lights that they could see came from the orange street lights on the outside of the park and, as they emerged from the treeline onto the football and rugby pitches, they saw nothing. Collins crouched down hoping to see the outline of somebody against these lights, but still they saw nothing. They ran on, keeping about twenty feet apart, close enough to corroborate each other's actions, but far enough apart not to both get hit, in a worst-case scenario.

They covered another hundred yards. Crouching down again, they could now see the building at the centre of the park that was illuminated by security lights, as it was constantly being broken into by some of the locals.

"There, Shug!" Jamie shouted as he spotted a figure outlined against the lights in the middle of the pitches, about a hundred yards in front of them. Standing up, he roared at the top of his voice, "Armed Police. Stand still!" The figure stopped, then turned and ran on. Collins and Beattie broke into a run too, managing to close the gap, but not close enough to stop him. Collins relayed a commentary as best he could over the radio, as he ran, "Target spotted heading southwards towards the building at the centre of the park, a hundred yards in front."

"Armed Police. Stand still!" Jamie bellowed again, and this time he turned on the tactical halogen light that was in place under the barrel of the G36. The powerful light showed their target clearly as they carried on running, still closing the gap. They could see the green jacket the male had been described as wearing.

After another few minutes, the suspect stopped. "Armed Police. Stand still," Jamie yelled a third time. "Show me your hands." He did not comply with the instruction but rather dropped to a knee, raising both hands in front of him.

Collins and Beattie were only thirty to forty yards from him now but could not make out clearly what he was holding, if anything. However, from his body position, it looked like he was preparing to shoot.

"Drop the fucking weapon!" Jamie hollered at him with real venom in his voice, as he clicked the safety catch off his G36. Both he and Collins then saw something drop at his side in the torch lights from their weapons, and he swung his arms out wide.

"Lie flat, arms out," Jamie instructed him and was pleased when he did as he was asked. Jamie stayed where he was, whilst Collins moved out at right angles to him, so that they would avoid the classic "blue-on-blue" – pointing their weapons at one another. Collins approached him from the side and kicked the metallic object away from his reach, all the while keeping his G36 trained on his target. As he drew near, he swung the weapon behind him and drew out his handcuffs, placing one cuff on the wrist as the man lay face down.

"Put your other hand into the small of your back," he said calmly, almost quietly. The man did as he was instructed, and Collins cinched up the other cuff securely on his other wrist.

"Secure," he shouted to Jamie, who joined him and then into his radio announced, "Male detained. Can we have transport, please?"

Beattie and Collins got the man to his feet and recovered the weapon, a good replica of a pistol, with a bar across the barrel that could only be seen in close examination by an experienced eye.

"What the fuck were you doing pointing that at us?" Beattie asked him but got no reply. "The one's we've got are real. You could've been shot."

"He nearly was," Collins chipped in. "I had the safety off when he dropped to one knee and raised his hands like that."

"So did I," Beattie replied. "I was shitting myself." And they both chuckled as their relief mechanism of laughing in the face of real danger kicked into gear, trying to dilute the adrenaline rushing through their bodies.

They walked the man over to the panda car that had arrived in the middle of the park, asking his name as they went but he never spoke. At the vehicle, they tried again for his details but received no response. Collins looked at his clothing in the light from the car and searched him. Pulling out his wallet revealed that he had a bank card with his name of it.

"There's your starter for ten" he laughed out loud, handing the bank card to the two officers escorting the prisoner. "You'd better formally detain him, though. We'll see you up there." He was placed into the vehicle and driven away. The local boys would finish the enquiry.

Beattie and Collins examined the recovered replica handgun and tied a green label around where the working parts retracted. The weapon now couldn't be closed properly, and it was obvious that it wasn't loaded. They both signed the label and gave everything to the local cops. Beattie and Collins were also finished, but they had to walk back to their car as the radios chattered with messages for sets to stand down all around. Back at their vehicle, they unloaded and wrote up their log of the incident from which they're actions would be recorded for the attention of senior officers. They then headed to the cells complex where they wrote out their statements for the detaining officers.

When finished, Collins said, "Come on, piece time, Jamie. We can do the incident report after piece," Collins said, "and besides, I've some calls to make"

They stopped off for chips on the way back to Police HQ and after eating and completing their paperwork, Collins phoned Willie Stuart on his mobile.

"Hi there, Willie. It's Shug. Are you free to speak?" he enquired.

"Aye, what can I do for you?"

"I was wondering how you got on with our wee enquiry and how your big enquiry is going. Have you solved it yet"? He asked cheerily, knowing that he would be in for a long slog.

"Well, it's like this. There's the ..." He stopped and started again, "We have the . . ." He stopped again. "It's the . . . No! Of course it's not solved," he laughed. "I did find out a little bit about our mutual friend, though. I had a wee look through his record and it seems he's been diagnosed with Asperger's Syndrome. That'll maybe account for him being such an arsehole. I also saw that he got a row off a boss for the thing you were talking about the other day."

"Well, I don't know much about Asperger's, but I do know that he's a cunt. There's no medicine for that."

"Yup, I think we can agree on that. We're getting nowhere fast with finding the killer, but we will. It'll take some time, but we'll get them. Have you anything to pass on?"

"We've just finished a job at Cameron Toll ..." he started but was interrupted by Stuart.

"Oh, aye. I was going to ask you about that. Do you know who it was?" he asked Collins.

"Somebody Henry, if I remember right. Sean Henry?"

"Sean Henry's the right-hand man of Ryan Docherty," Stuart interjected.

"Well, it seems like he was dishing out a warning to Buchan's crew that Ryan wants to be in charge. He was knocking lumps out of someone at Liberton Rugby Club when he was interrupted. There's been no complaints made, as you would expect," Collins continued.

"Your war for control has started then, Willie?"

"Aye, it looks like it has. There'll be more to come. This is just the opening salvo."

Collins then relayed the information that he had obtained from the shooting estate and how he had come by it.

"You've got the makings of a detective about you, Shug," Stuart replied, obviously impressed by Collins' thinking outside of the box.

"And that got me thinking," Collins continued. "There was a fingerprint found at the locus of the HB when Harry Kings' rifle was stolen, but it's not been identified yet. What if it's Neilson's?"

"Yes, that just crossed my mind, too. But the ID branch wouldn't search through the fingerprints of serving cops. They're just taken for elimination purposes and can't be routinely searched. You need to have pre-cons for your prints to be searched," Stuart agreed.

"Can we not just get the ID branch to do that, though?" Collins asked innocently

"No, we can't. But let me ask you: Are you alone right now?"

"Aye, why? What is it?"

Stuart had thought long and hard about whether he should tell Collins about his name coming up in the enquiry. He was usually an excellent judge of character but this new evidence had thrown him. If he didn't tell him, Collins would be extremely pissed off, and rightly so. If he did tell him, and he was involved, then he'd just fucked up the enquiry, big time! But he had trusted his instincts.

"You ain't gonna like this. But your name's come up in our enquiry, and Neilson wants to have you brought in."

"What for?" Collins gulped. "What do you mean, 'brought in'?"

"Detained, as part of the enquiry."

"What the fuck for?"

"I don't know. Perverting the course of justice or something. You came up after the ID Branch found your DNA on a cigar at the locus. You're also a firearms certificate holder for a .308 rifle, and you were at the locus."

"Of course I was at the fucking locus," Collins almost shouted down the phone and then, realising where he was, changed his tone.

"Of course I was at the locus," he repeated. "I was on the firearms response to the murder and was put out the back of the home by one of your guys, Laura Fraser."

"I know, I know. Don't shoot the messenger," he said, laughing at his unintended pun. "I told him that and explained everything as you've just done, but he wants you seen sooner rather than later, you know, like anyone else whose name crops up," Stuart said, trying to calm Collins down in his righteous anger.

"How can they not look at cops' fingerprints but they can look at their DNA?" Collins asked.

"It's just one big national database, Shug. Feed in the information and act on what you get back out. But what you've said is interesting because Neilson was head of Professional Standards when the HB was done on the farmhouse. Any memo to access cops prints would have to go through him before it got to the Deputy Chief."

"So it could be his print at Hawick, but we don't know because he blocked it."

"Or something like that, yes. But we really don't know whose print it is, at all, do we?" Stuart replied and then asked, "Now, about your .308. Could you bring it into the murder squad so that it can be examined? We're checking up on everybody who has one, anyway. If you were to bring it down here, we could put an end to this nonsense, once and for all. You can explain easily why you were there and your rifle isn't going to be the murder weapon, is it?"

"You're a very persuasive man, Inspector," Collins said and Stuart could sense that he had calmed his colleague's furore. "Is tomorrow too soon?"

"No, that would be great. I'll not be there, which is even better. It'll not look like we're in cahoots."

"Where are you going, then?" Collins asked.

"I'm off to find Docherty and give him a hard time. Your pal Laura Fraser's going to come along. Very astute young lady, that, and she's on the squad, anyway."

"I'm backshift again tomorrow, anyway, Willie. I'll chuck my gun in the back of the car and come down."

"Alrighty," Willie answered. "Keep your powder dry tomorrow and mind what you say."

"Aye, aye. I will do, Willie. Sorry about blowing up, there." Collins apologised.

"Don't worry about it. I'll be in touch. Cheers, Shug." Stuart said, hanging up the phone.

"Fucking bastard," Collins said under his breath. "One of these days, I'm gonna nail him."

Chapter Eleven

Dick Neilson was already at his desk when Willie Stuart walked into murder squad office the following morning.

"Morning, Boss," he said, as he stuck his head around the door to see that Neilson was already pouring over sheets and sheets of paper, updating himself with the results of enquiries that had been completed and those which were still outstanding.

"You've started early."

"Ah, Willie. The very man." Neilson said. "I need a quick word. Come in. Take a seat and shut the door."

Stuart did as he was asked and sat down opposite his boss.

"Yes, what can I do for you?"

"I've been thinking about what you said yesterday about this cop -- Oh, what's his name?" as he shuffled the papers on his desk, apparently looking for the name. "Ah, yes. Here it is. Hugh Collins."

Good effort, Stuart thought to himself, *but not worthy of an Oscar in the acting stakes.* Stuart knew that Neilson was perfectly aware of the name of the officer, but he went along with the pretence. "Aye, what about him?"

"Well, I think it's best that I interview him. I'm the ranking officer here and I'm used to being involved in disciplinary matters."

"But like I said yesterday, Boss, this isn't a disciplinary matter. It's a murder enquiry. I don't think that we should be getting side-tracked with stuff like this. We've much bigger fish to fry."

"I know that, Willie. But he's caused us and the ID Branch to waste time examining items that he's dropped at a crime scene. I feel that he should be brought in and questioned about that."

"But we've been doing that with everything found. Everybody to date has had a perfectly good reason for being there, be they staff, residents, or visitors. Nobody else has had to be 'brought in.' This guy is no different from anyone else and he's certainly not the first cop to contaminate a murder scene. He certainly won't be the last," Stuart suggested, remembering previous crime scenes that he had been at throughout his service, where cops and detectives had touched things or picked up items that should've been left well alone.

Then there were the footprints. That was one of the main reasons that a crime scene log was compiled at the earliest opportunity and why Stuart had always resorted to putting his hands in his pockets at a crime scene. It perhaps looked bad when he and others did it, but it served a very good purpose.

"That's beside the point, Willie. I've sent him an email already and asked him to come in here today. He's backshift, I think?" He looked at Stuart directly, his dark eyes unblinking, seeking some sort of reaction. *Was this a test?* Stuart thought, but he was far too shrewd a detective to give away his thoughts that easily. He just looked back at Neilson without expression, giving nothing away.

"Did you ask him to bring in his rifle, too? May as well kill two birds with the one stone. We can get it sent to the ballistics boys to have a look at it," he suggested.

"No, I didn't but that would be a good idea. I'll do that."

"But he's not going to get the email until he comes on duty later and he wouldn't have the rifle with him, would he?"

"Yes, well, I'll send it anyway. I think it's important that I'm seen to be getting involved, don't you?"

"It's your enquiry. You're the boss. I'm going to be out this afternoon. There's a couple of things need bottomed out with the house hits the other day. I want to try and get the word out on the street again. Let's see what we can get back."

Stuart busied himself about the office for the rest of the morning, but as events transpired, Laura Fraser was out on an enquiry when he left the office, intending on tracing Ryan Docherty.

Later that day, Hugh Collins and Jamie Beattie were ready to get out on the road in the ARV and drove straight to the murder squad offices. Collins had placed his own rifle in its carrying case in the back of the vehicle and it wasn't long before he pulled up in the station car park. They had spoken about why Collins had to be there, obviously, but he hadn't spoken about his conversations with Willie Stuart.

"Grab yourself a coffee, Jamie. This shouldn't take long," he said, as he walked into the squad office with the rifle slung over his shoulder.

He spoke with the first person he saw, identified himself, and explained the reason for his being there.

"I thought it best that I come down here now. You'd want to speak to me anyway and have a look at this," he said, as he shrugged his shoulder carrying the rifle.

"Aye, we would" the detective agreed. "I'll take you to the boss. It's him that wants to speak to you."

He was shown into Neilson's empty office, and he took a seat, propping his rifle against the wall. He sat for several minutes waiting before Neilson entered with another officer who Collins didn't recognise.

Collins didn't get up. *Fucking typical,* he thought. *He keeps me waiting because he can. Not because he's busy.*

"Hello, Dick," he said.

"That's DCI Neilson, Constable Collins!" Neilson cut him short, obviously annoyed at his informality to his seniority.

"Yeah, okay. Sorry about that, Chief Inspector. You wanted to see me?"

"Indeed. I'm SIO of this murder enquiry, as you may know, and you've been identified as someone who was at the crime scene."

"Yes"

"What were you there for?"

"You know why I was there. It'll be on the log for the job," Collins responded, deadpan and in monotone.

"Yes, but I'd like to hear it from you."

"I was on the cordon with the firearms teams for most of the night."

"How long were you there for?"

"No idea. It'll be on the log."

"Who were you with?"

"I can't remember. A young cop from this station. It'll be on the log."

"Where were you on the cordon?"

"Out the back of the home, as per Laura Fraser's instruction,"

Neilson shuffled several sheets of paper backwards and forwards, looking for some information. Finding what he had been looking for, he asked, "I've checked back on the intelligence system. It seems that you have been accessing Buchan's records. Why did you do that?"

"I'm a cop. It's my job to see what he's been doing or suspected of doing, who he hangs about with, et cetera."

"But why just him?"

"It's not just him. I try to keep on top of the intelligence coming in about him and all the rest of the bad guys. I might have to deal with him again one day. Did you look for any other entries that I've had a look at, relating to his associates or opposition, or any of the hundreds of others things that are going on?"

"Why would you be dealing with him?" Neilson asked in an almost derogatory manner.

"You mean a major player in the drugs game, with access to firearms, should be of no interest to me?" Collins retorted straight back with as much sarcasm as he could manage.

"I see you've brought your rifle in today. It's a .308, isn't it?" said Neilson, changing the subject hastily.

"Correct."

"Who told you to bring it in? You wouldn't have got my email until you came on duty."

"Nobody told me. I just figured that you'd want to speak to everyone on the firearms register who's owns a rifle."

"How did you know we were looking for someone with a .308 rifle?"

"Wait a minute, Chief Inspector. Am I suspected of something, here? If I am, I should be cautioned and you should explain to me what I'm suspected of," Collins said, leaning forwards, with obvious irritation in his voice.

Neilson was annoyed at Collins' outburst and knew that he was now on the back foot. He was now answering questions instead of asking them. Flustered, he tried to maintain his composure.

"No, no," he replied slowly, thinking for his next move. "It's just procedures."

"So you're thinking that I've somehow broken procedures?"

"No, it's not that …" Neilson replied, stumbling over his words.

"Well, in that case, if it's a disciplinary matter," he pressed on, "I'll give you an operational statement about what I did on the night and that'll be that. You can make your investigations …"

"Hugh," the DS interrupted, "this is just to establish who was there and why they were there. You're right. We are looking at everyone who owns a registered rifle. This is normal for a murder enquiry. We need to eliminate the obvious when we don't have positive leads. No one is accusing you of anything."

"Okay, then. To answer your question," he said, returning his attention to Neilson, "I didn't know you were looking for someone with a .308 or 7.62 mm rifle, but they're pretty common. Probably the most-used weapon in the world for deer."

"And you shoot for deer, do you?" Neilson interjected, happy that he was now back in control of the interview after being bailed out by his sergeant.

"I have done, yes. But I also use it for vermin control on a couple of farms that give me permission. I can give you their names if you want them. By all means, send my gun to HQ for testing. That's why I brought it in. It's not the weapon that you're looking for."

"One last thing, then," Neilson asked, "why did you drop a cigar butt in my crime scene?"

"I didn't know I was in your crime scene. I asked DS Fraser for the approximate distances for the initial cordon, and I was on the outside of that. I had a smoke. So what?"

They sat staring at each other for a few seconds and then Neilson looked away at his sergeant.

"Anything else to add?" he asked the DS, breaking the silence.

"No, I think you've covered it," the DS replied. "We'll get your rifle back to you as soon as we can, Hugh. Thanks for coming in."

"No problem," Collins responded to him, not even looking at Neilson as he got up and left the office.

"Well, that went well, don't you think?" Neilson asked the DS after Collins had left. The DS wasn't sure if Neilson was trying to make a joke or not.

"Just peachy," he retorted and left to return to his duties.

Whilst Collins was being interviewed, Willie Stuart had been out and about in his old stomping ground of Gracemount. He knew Ryan Docherty from long ago and had watched as he had moved up in the world in his chosen, albeit illegal, profession. Stuart knew what was going to happen after Buchan had been removed from the scene. He had seen it all too often.

Sitting in his car outside Docherty's house, he remembered that, before Buchan had managed to bludgeon his way to the top through violence and intimidation of those around him, he had been a loyal lieutenant for the previous top dog. When he had died, a war for the control of the drugs trade in the south side of the city had begun. The southsiders began fighting amongst themselves with several factions grouping together, inflicting severe beatings on others, bribing them with promised riches, or relying on long-standing loyalties in order to establish their supremacy.

No one had been safe and several times, bystanders had been caught in the middle when one faction had sought out a rival and beat him with baseball bats to within an inch of his life. There were obviously no witnesses to these events, even though many people had seen what had happened and were well aware of what was going on. They were just too afraid to pick a side. Into the mix had come the northsiders who, seeing that there was a power vacuum, had tried to take advantage of the in-fighting. Sending their teams south to attempt to seize control of the trade for the whole of Edinburgh, dishing out beatings to the weaker links had resulted in reciprocal visits to the north.

It had not been a happy time for a young cop who had seen first-hand the injuries sustained by the victims – kneecaps smashed with hammers or the many stabbings. An old cop had described it to him as "shite fighting with shite" at the time and, to a certain extent, Stuart had agreed.

But over the years, as he got to know some of the people and learned that they had wives, girlfriends, and kids, he now understood that, as Robert Burns had written, "A man's a man fur aw' that" – everybody was the same and wanted the same for their families. They just went about it in different ways. He had treated them with respect in his dealings with them and had, in turn, earned their respect as someone who played the game straight and always did what he said he would do.

But lately, he was beginning to doubt that that had been the right way to go. He had joined the police hoping to make a difference and fought against a natural descent into cynicism after being lied to by so many people for so many years. But there was always someone who was ready to step into the shoes left by the previous player and the game went on. There was no end to it, and it was beginning to take its toll on him.

Why not fight fire with fire? Stuart had thought many times. *They have no rules to play by, whilst we have to fight with one hand tied behind our backs. They complain to the authorities about every action we take against them; complain about comments made. The smallest mistake is amplified in Court by lawyers, making out that you are a liar, inept, or have acted illegally. Maybe Henry VI was right, when Shakespeare had him say, "The first thing we do. Let's kill all the lawyers."*

He was well-aware that the pistol-whipping dished out by Sean Henry was only the start of Ryan Docherty's grab for power.

Stuart had called on a couple of the names that he had recognised from the notebook that Collins had found, and had asked if he could speak with Docherty. He hadn't expected to actually speak to him but knew that the "bush telegraph" would start ringing and the people that he had visited would soon be on the phone to Docherty telling him that the police were looking for him. He had left a mobile phone number with them, and it wasn't long before his phone rang.

"Mr Stuart?" He recognised Docherty's voice at once.

"Ah, Doc, thanks for calling me back," he replied, using Docherty's nickname. "I'd like to speak to you if you've got nothing on. Nothing formal you understand," he said, conscious about not putting Docherty's guard up. "Just a wee chat. Nothing heavy."

"What do you want to chat about, like?" Docherty came back at him, obviously wary.

"Well, I might have something that would interest you, and you might have something that would be of use to me."

"Aye, okay, then. Just you and me?"

"Just you and me, Doc. Usual place? Say, in an hour?"

"Aye, I can do that"

Stuart had spoken with Docherty many times over the years and had never registered him as one of his "touts" because he wasn't and never would be. Informants were paid but had to be registered as such in case money went missing. This was a personal arrangement. A "professional courtesy."

The usual place was a car park off the A702 heading towards the Scottish borders, near Flotterston, that was popular with hill walkers wishing to tramp the Pentland hills on the south side of Edinburgh. There were many well-worn tracks and trails that could be followed by the more ambitious walker or, for the less fit, a tarmac road that lead to a couple of lochs where trout fishing was also popular.

The important thing was that mobile reception was limited and it was off the beaten track, having also been the scene of a double murder, or rather an execution, many years previously when an army payroll had been stolen and the culprit had simply killed the witnesses to his actions. The money stolen had never been recovered and rumour had it that for years afterwards, in the summer months, families would go picnicking in the hills, taking a spade with them - just on the off chance that they might stumble over something. That murder had been Stuart's introduction to a large enquiry as a young detective.

Docherty didn't take an hour to arrive at the car park. He was en route almost as soon as he had hung up the phone. He wanted to get there early and have a good look around, just to satisfy himself that they would not be under surveillance and, sure enough, on arrival, saw that the car park was almost empty. There was a chill in the air and a cold wind was blowing. Not very good for walking.

Docherty parked up in a corner of the car park opposite the exit, ready in case he had to leave quickly. He had known Willie Stuart for years and had been locked up by him several times over those years, but he carried a grudging respect for him. He had never double-crossed him when he had supplied a little snippet of information or when he had admitted to additional crimes in order to gain his liberty. Some cops, he was well aware, would get a few jobs out of an individual on the promise of being released for a summons to Court at a later date, only to be locked up anyway. Willie Stuart was an okay guy – for a bizzie.

After a short wait, Docherty saw a car draw into the car park with Stuart at the wheel, and he saw that he was alone. Parking a short distance away, he watched as Stuart got out of the car, holding his coat closed against himself with his hands, before walking over to him. Ryan got out his car, met with him in the middle.

"Mr Stuart," he said again, "long time no see, I'm happy to say," with a grin.

"Aye, it's been a few years. How are you doing?"

"Aye, okay."

"Listen, it's fucking Baltic up here. Can we get out of this wind?" Stuart suggested.

"Where you want to go?"

"I'm not bothered. Just out of the wind so we can hear each other talk."

Docherty suggested walking over to the public toilets, which although closed, would provide shelter in the lea of the building.

"What do you want, Mr Stuart?"

"How did you get on in Court the other day?"

"Not guilty. They never found anything, anyway. Just a wee bit of personal," referring to the cannabis roaches, reefer butts, which had been found in his house. "I'll get a wee fine, according to my lawyer."

"Well, on that subject, you'll know that we found some good information."

"Did you?" Docherty posed the question, well aware of what Stuart was talking about. He had gone to his hiding place under the carpet as soon as he had got home. His heart had sank when he saw his notebook was gone but took comfort in the fact that he had put it in code.

"Aye, we did. Makes interesting reading, too."

"Does it?"

"Pretty smart, Ryan, pretty smart. I remember when you joined the navy. But you know you shouldn't've written it down in any format. If Matty had known you'd done that, he wouldn't've been a happy boy."

"I've no' got the memory that he's got. He remembers everything."

"He does, he does," Stuart agreed. "But now we know, too, and we both know what is going to happen next. There's going to be a fight for who takes his place. You're well-placed, for sure, but there'll be a lot of unhappy people if it gets out that you've dropped them in the shite."

He offered Docherty a cigarette, which he accepted. They both lit up and pulled on their smokes, allowing the silence to develop, each thinking what their next step would be. Docherty had already worked out that he had some bridges to build and that he had burned some beyond repair. He had already started to try to limit the damage that had been caused, and he knew that Stuart knew it, too.

"We're toiling with the enquiry, Ryan," Stuart broke the silence. "Whoever done it was good. He's left very little for us to go on. We've got a few leads but I would appreciate it if you could give us a wee steer, here and there."

"I don't know who did it, Mr Stuart. You know there's loads of folk who would like to do him in."

"Aye, there is that. But you're on the inside and you know how the game is played. I've always played it straight, too, and I'm being upfront with you. I'm not asking you about his money or his stash or the folk who work for him. I've got a murder to solve. That's all I'm interested in."

"I'm no' a grass, Mr Stuart," Docherty replied flatly.

"I know you're not. But if it's someone from your side, we can lock him up and he's out of the picture. If it's someone from the north side, then they get the jail and they're away, as well. It'll be one less person that you've got to worry about or deal with. I take it it's started?" he asked, referring to Sean Henry again.

"No' yet, really," Docherty replied, knowing full well what Stuart was talking about. "But folk are asking questions and they're taking sides. Is it just folk in the business that you want or others, too?" Docherty asked.

"I'll take anything that you can give me. You and Matty go a long way back. I'm sure that you'd want his killer caught."

"The boy on the inside?" Docherty offered. Stuart's mind raced and he was conscious about not giving away any outward appearance of having been surprised, but he was. He thought to himself, *Does he mean the cop from the Crime Squad who had been trying to infiltrate Buchan crime group or does he mean Neilson?*

"The boy on the inside?" he asked, as innocently as he could manage.

"Aye, the cop boss who was at school with Matty."

"Who's that, then?"

"The boy Neilson. Matty's had him in his pocket for years. I've never met him, but I know he was getting money from Matty."

"What for?"

"Information about what you guys knew about him. Information about the opposition. Stuff like that. He used to get me the money to pay him but, like I said, I never met him. I'd drop the cash off somewhere and he would pick it up. Matty never said who he was. I thought it was a fake name."

"I've never heard of him either, Ryan," he lied convincingly. "How did Matty get in touch with him?"

"The phone, probably, but I don't know the number. Matty would phone me and tell me that he wanted some money dropped off for Neilson, and I'd do it pretty soon after that. Didn't want to get caught with cash in the house and get a hard time off him, or you lot, did I?"

"Where did you drop off the money?"

"Train station, usually. I have a key to one of the boxes there. I'd drop off the money, and he would pick it up sometime after that."

"Always the same box?"

"Aye."

"Fair enough, Ryan. But I'll tell you this. Keep your ears open for anything that might help me and we'll call it quits. That'll be us square. How about that?"

"Aye, fair enough. But, like I said, I have no idea who done Matty in."

"Okay, then," Stuart replied "but if I find out that this is a load of shite or you are involved, then you know what will happen."

"Aye, I know."

They said their goodbyes and each drove off from the car park wondering if they had given too much away. Stuart was already thinking that he had to speak with Shug. Ryan hadn't solved his murder case but he had helped in building a case against Neilson. Or so he hoped.

Chapter Twelve

Stuart got back to the office in mid-afternoon to be told that there may have been a breakthrough in the case. The DS who had sat in on the interview with Hugh Collins and Neilson updated him as to how it had panned out.

"Neilson started out badly and got worse, Willie," he told his boss. "He didn't really have a plan of what he wanted to ask and he went about it in an overbearing and dictatorial manner that just got the boy Collins' back up. He gave as good as he got, though. Do they have some history together?"

"Pass. I don't know him," he had lied again, something that was becoming more common and which he didn't like about himself. He had always been upfront and honest in his dealings with everybody throughout his service.

"Anyway, Willie, it looks like we might have a bit of a lead in our wee job. The guys who've been watching the CCTV videos for the last week have turned something up," and he offered him a print taken from the video. Stuart took it and saw a grainy, black and white image of a male, dressed in black trousers, with what looked like black boots, with a bulky coat over the top. The image had been taken in the dark against the backdrop of the orange street light.

"Where did you get this?" he asked.

"It's from the council CCTV on Old Dalkeith Road near Ferniehill at the bottom of the Wisp."

"And what's so special about it that makes you think he's involved?"

"Well, here's another image of him carrying a case."

Stuart looked at another blurred image but could make out the shape of a case that he was carrying.

"It doesn't look like a briefcase -- too big for that, I would suggest. It's certainly not a suitcase or a holdall either. It looks like a hard-shell case. But what is really strange is that he just disappears off the radar afterwards. I've had the guys checking the cameras north and south of where this was taken, and he can't be found. They're checking the cameras in the housing estates now in case he's gone home or whatever. And another thing," the DS continued, "it was taken about seven on the night in question."

"Alrighty, we need to get these images enhanced in some way. You know, more definition," Stuart said.

"I've already done that. I've made arrangements to get the video taken down to the technical guys to see what they can do."

"Do we have any cameras in The Wisp area? What's there?"

"When I was first told about the images, I went up there. The Wisp runs basically east and west from the east side of Craigmillar over the top of the hill towards Old Dalkeith Road. The camera that got these images is at the top end of the Wisp on Old Dalkeith Road, at the junction with it, in fact. There's cameras monitoring traffic flow southwards that we're looking at right now, as well as cameras going northwards past the new Royal Infirmary. There'll be loads of cameras at the junction of the city bypass. Old Dalkeith Road joins it there about a couple of miles down the road. The Wisp itself has houses on the east side but there's open farm land with a few trees and copses dotted around. I think there's cattle in the fields."

"Good stuff," Stuart said.

"The top of the Wisp also gives you a great view over to Craigmillar Castle, and it also looks out over the university playing fields and the back of the home," the DS said in a matter-of-fact way, allowing his boss to draw his own conclusions.

"Does it, now? That's interesting" he said as he looked up from the images to the DS, opening his eyes just that little wider, raising his eyebrows. They both knew what the other was thinking.

"Aye, that's what I thought," the DS responded.

"Can we get these images enhanced as soon as possible? Black and white if we have to. Colour would be better. Can you get them to see if they can get anything to give us a comparison with? You know, something that we could estimate his height or size of build, that type of thing. Can we get some of the guys who're in the office right now onto watching the CCTV tapes to find out where this guy --" Willie waved the sheet of paper bearing the images, "--went to? Can we also put it out to the local uniform boys? See if they know him, if he's a local?"

"I don't think there's any more TVs that they can use, Boss."

"Have we got all the footage from the cameras around that area?"

"We don't have it all. I was waiting for the okay from you or the DCI, but I've made the necessary arrangements to get it or at least have it kept. It's usually kept for a month, I'm told."

"For fuck's sake," Stuart replied, "that's annoying. Right. Get your hands on all the footage from any cameras around the area. Say, from six until nine on the night." He could never be criticised for not making a decision.

"Has the DCI been updated? You know how he moans about being kept in the loop?"

"Yeah, I told him, but he didn't seem that interested, really. Said something like it's a guy walking home from the office and didn't look like much because they were crap pictures," the DS replied with just a hint of scorn.

"Well, he could be going home and they are crap images. But who wears boots to and from the office. We'll need to find out who he is."

"You think we should get a search team up to the Wisp to have a look?"

"It's been a couple of weeks now. There'll have been joggers going past, farmers going in and out of the fields, cars going up and down …" Stuart responded.

"I think so," the DS agreed.

Stuart went into his office again, sat, and then reclined in his chair with his eyes closed – his favoured thinking position – when Neilson walked in.

"Ah, you're back," he said.

"I am, indeed, Boss."

"Have you heard about my interview with Collins?"

"Yeah, somebody mentioned he'd been in."

"I think he's hiding something."

"Really?" Stuart responded as he sat up in his chair. "What makes you say that?"

"He's just too cocky. Too confident. Brought in a rifle – his own rifle -- for us to examine. It could be anybody's."

"Well, I feel confident that the firearms licensing will check that it's his rifle, Boss."

"Yes, but he could easily have another one. One that he's not supposed to have."

"He could, yes. But then so could anyone out there. And we haven't even started on the squaddies who might have something illegal. How did you get on with the military police?"

"They haven't got back to me yet."

"Let's see how that pans out, then. That and this image of the guy in black with a case."

"I don't think that it's worthy of much, Willie."

"On the face of it, no," he had to agree, "but if he's disappeared like a fart in the wind, we'll have to find out why and where he went and who he is. We can't rule anyone out, can we?"

"Including Collins," Neilson said forcefully.

"Including Collins," Stuart agreed.

With that, Neilson was gone. *Jesus. He really hates you, Shug,* he thought to himself and then remembered that he was going to phone Collins.

Taking his own mobile, he dialled Collins' personal mobile, checking his watch as the phone tried to connect. *Four pm. He should be on duty. Hopefully not busy.*

"Hello," Collins answered.

"Shug? It's Willie. Are you free to speak?"

"Aye, I'm off at the West End Station making safe some bullets that have been handed in. How the hell you make a bullet safe is beyond me. Just dinny fire it, I would suggest."

"Who asked you to do that?"

"Some arse of a sergeant here thought it best if we tied one of our green labels around the bullets."

"They're not .308 or 7.62 millimetre, are they?" Stuart laughed.

"No, they're not. They're .50 calibre on a webbing belt, fifteen of them. Old as the hills, too. Probably from a Spitfire or something like that from the war. They were found in an old flat that's getting renovated. Anyway, what can I do for you?"

"Right, I spoke with Doc. I told you about it. He's confirmed that our other wee enquiry is right. Your pal has been getting money via him as per the notebook. You follow me?" he asked, conscious not to use Ryan Docherty's name.

"Yeah, I think so," Collins replied, picking up the gist of the information that Stuart was trying to pass him.

"I think I'm right in saying that Doc's SIM card will have kept all the calls made and calls received from whichever phone it was put in. If the details are there, we could cross-reference the dates when Ryan had the money for your pal. That way, we might be able to get Neilson's phone number confirmed. That, and Buchan's."

"I think you are right, Willie. I should have thought about that the other night. I'll get on with it tomorrow. I'm backshift tonight and tomorrow. I'll do a bit in the morning, and I'm days off again after that."

"Good enough, mate. Oh, and by the way, you don't have more than one rifle, do you?"

"No, why?" Collins asked, confused.

"Oh, it's just something your pal mentioned today. Nothing to worry about."

Chapter Thirteen

It had taken Collins most of the following morning and some of his day off to obtain the information they were looking for. Taking Docherty's SIM card and inserting it into his own phone again, he was able to access its contacts list without any trouble, and these numbers he knew he had already written down. They consisted of several low-level soldiers that most cops knew were involved in the drugs trade.

Docherty wasn't stupid enough to plumb everyone's name into a mobile phone. However, this time Collins flicked through the calls-made menu and he carefully noted the numbers, the contact details, where they were recorded, along with dates and times the calls had been made. He then did the same with calls that had been received to the SIM card and, for good measure, he accessed the answer phone, but without success.

There were many calls listed, but using the list of contact numbers that he and Stuart had compiled, Collins compared the lists of calls made and received, looking for similarities in the numbers on the lists on or around the same dates. It wasn't long before the frequency of the same repeated numbers became obvious. A call was received on Docherty's phone a couple of days prior to him making a call back to that number and was always on or about the day which the notebook confirmed that Neilson had been given money.

That must be Docherty's mobile, then, Collins thought. *He must be calling back to confirm the money had been dropped off.*

When he phoned Stuart with the results of what he had found, he had sounded disappointed.

"Hmm, I thought that we might have been able to get a phone number for Neilson."

"Yes, that was what I was hoping for, as well, but I thought you said that Docherty had only ever been contacted by Buchan and that Docherty had never met Neilson, only dropped off cash at Waverley Station. There are a few calls made and received on Docherty's mobile. The number he called around the dates when the notebook says Neilson got money must be Buchan's mobile."

"You're right, Shug. I think I'm getting a wee bit punch drunk with all that is going on in my head right now."

"So if this number is Buchan's, where do we go from here?" Collins asked.

"Well, we have to confirm the number somehow." Stuart suggested. "If we want to access the phone records from the company, we'll have to go through a super for the authority to do it."

"Aye, but this if different, Willie," Collins chipped in. "This is part of your murder enquiry, not, on the face of it at least, anything to do with internal corruption."

"Christ, you're right. I am losing the plot."

"Did Buchan have the phone on him when he was shot? It might be lying with his personal possessions at the mortuary," Collins suggested.

"No, it's not there. I went through his possessions when I was at the post-mortem."

"That's a shame. I could've given him a bell and left a message for you." They both chuckled down the line with each other.

"I'll tell you what I'm going to do. I'll submit an authorisation through our superintendent to access what we think is Buchan's phone records. More than likely, it'll be a pay-as-you-go phone, without a contract, but they'll still have records."

With a contract phone, the mobile telephone companies entered into business with their customers providing a service for an agreed upon time, after which a phone was upgraded and a new contract signed. With a pay-as-you go agreement, there was no contract and the service provider would not have any details of the owner of the phone. They would still have details of the calls made and received, however.

"We'll just have to trust our instincts on this one, Shug, and believe that the phone number is Buchan's. What's the company, by the way?"

"O2, Willie."

"Okay, then, I'll get that squared away and let you know how it goes."

"Cheers, Willie," Collins said, as a thank you for the update, as well as a goodbye.

Stuart sat back in his chair again and thought about what he would say to his bosses regarding where he had gotten this information from. It would have to be bland, he knew, but worth following up in order to obtain the super's signature.

As he sat at the computer terminal typing up the required forms, one of the DS's poked his head around the door.

"Willie? You're gonna love this."

"Oh, really? Is it a pint or a large whiskey?"

"Maybe later. I've just picked up a wee note, an email, from a couple of the uniform boys. It seems that they were out and about on the night of the murder when they stumbled over an old car parked up off the main drag in The Wisp. The guy says that they regularly check that area, as it's a dumping ground for stolen cars. Some of the locals burn them up out there. They thought it a bit strange that there was a car parked there and had a look. It was all locked up and it didn't look like it had been stolen – you know, the steering column was intact, no windows were smashed, and it wasn't on fire," he said with a wry smile.

"When was this? What time?"

"Between about half-seven and eight."

"And this is the bit you said overlooks the fields at the back of the locus?"

"That's the one, yes."

"And the registration number is?"

"Ah, that's where it goes a bit tits-up, I'm afraid. They said they ran a check on the number plate and it came back as unregistered, scrapped, or exported, but they got called away to deal with something else. It was bonfire night, after all, and the fire service were taking in-coming," the DS said, referring to the fire service always being busy on the 5th November putting out the illegal bonfires that many people up and down the country went to. When the fire services began to put out the fires, local youths sometimes began throwing stones or shooting fireworks at them, and this caused the police no end of trouble.

"When they got back to the car later in the evening, it had gone."

"Dog walker?" Stuart suggested.

"In the arse end of Craigmillar and on bonfire night?" the DS sounded confused. Stuart could see immediately that it had been a stupid remark, but he was exhausted and needing a good, long, uninterrupted night of sleep -- something that he had not had since the murder had happened.

"Of course," he said, almost embarrassed. The DS could sense his boss's uneasiness.

"Don't worry about it. We're all fucked."

"Right, then. Where do we go from here, then?" he asked. *Perhaps he should let someone else do the thinking,* he thought, knowing that his DS had probably considered what to do next, anyway.

"Okay. We don't have the registration number, but it's an old Ford Fiesta, green in colour. I'll get the guys to check back all the vehicles that were checked out on the night of 5th November from the PNC and we should be able to get it that way. We have the cops' collar numbers so it shouldn't take too long to get it."

The Police National Computer held all the details of vehicles registered in the UK, together with details of insurance and test certificates, should they exist.

"I love it when a plan comes together. Can you let the DCI know what we've got?"

"Will do, Willie" he said as he spun on his heels and left the office.

We're getting warmer, Stuart thought to himself as he finished typing up the forms for the super and then wandered through to get a coffee. He needed caffeine and nicotine, he thought, as he walked to the back door of the station where he lit up a cigarette. As he stood there smoking and drinking his coffee, Neilson came outside to join him.

"What's this about a car?" he asked.

"Have you just been told? That seems to be good news."

"I don't think we should be chasing ghosts, Willie. A parked car means nothing."

"We won't know until we find out, though, will we?"

"Well, I should've been told first so that I can make these decisions. It's going to involve a fair bit of additional resources, to say nothing of the time and money involved."

"Resources, time, money," Stuart repeated. "I'm sorry, but what the fuck do I care about that. This is a crime. This is a murder enquiry that we're trying to solve here."

"But we're still looking at the information that we got from people who were there at the time. There's the ID branch stuff to wade through and to follow up, the firearms register enquiries to get through, the background stuff that we have to get about Buchan, as well as all the CCTV that has to be viewed. I don't think that we should be going off at tangents, down what is more than likely a dead end, all on the information from two young uniformed cops."

"I think you're wrong," Willie told him flatly. "This is a positive lead. Loads of these street cops are shit hot with stuff like this."

"That's as may be. I've told you what I think and I'm the SIO. Don't put the information into the system until we've finished what we're doing already."

Stuart was not in the mood to argue. Taking a last drag on his cigarette, he flicked the butt into a nearby bucket and then blew the smoke out, sighing as he did so.

"You're the boss, Boss, but you'll have to explain later why this wasn't followed up straight away, bearing in mind we've got the boy dressed in black at the end of the street who just disappeared."

"Are you challenging my authority?"

"No, I'm not challenging your authority, but the super and the PF will want to know when you update them, that's all. And if the car is involved . . ." He trailed off and allowed Neilson to draw his own conclusions before walking back into the station, leaving him standing. Neilson felt beads of sweat appear on his forehead despite the cold, and the self-doubt inside him raced through his mind again *What if I am asked these questions? What do I say?*

Fucking dick, right enough! Stuart thought as he walked past him back into the station. *Limited imagination, repetitive behaviour, dislike of change. That's his Asperger's talking.*

Stuart dove into the toilets on his way back to his office, giving Neilson enough time, he thought, to get back to his office. After washing his hands, he found his DS again.

"Neilson's put the kibosh on your lead. Don't put it into the system . . . yet. Do the enquiry and let me know what the outcome is. Don't tell him, though," he said, nodding in the direction of Neilson's office. The DS looked baffled, and Stuart saw his confusion.

"I know, I know," he said in a matter of fact way, "one hand tied behind our back."

Stuart went back into his office and resumed his thinking position.

Why? he asked himself. *Why is he blocking what looks like a good lead? It can't just be Asperger's or that he's mixed up with Buchan. He has got something to hide but is there something else? Something that I've not considered or thought about?*

He sat up again and printed off a copy of his typed form, folded it, and stuck it into his jacket pocket. He then sent a copy to Superintendent McInnes who had oversight of the enquiry.

Him and I go back a long way, he thought. *He'll trust my judgement in wanting to know who's been in contact with Buchan shortly before he was killed. He'll know where I'm going with this.*

Midway through his thought process, he stopped himself again.

What if McInnes mentions it to Neilson in one of their update chats? I've sent it from my personal email account so the reply won't go back to the squad group email account. What if Neilson does find out and gets rid of his phone? Well, hopefully the enquiry will be done before that. It'll be sent directly onwards to the Communications Technical Department anyway, and if that happens, I'll still have Neilson's phone records and he'll be fucked.

Chapter Fourteen

Stuart needed some time off. He knew from past experience that he was burning himself out. He had hardly seen or spoken to his wife since the enquiry had started and, apart from one round of golf, he'd had no time to himself. He was feeling the effects of the long working days and restless nights, when he tossed and turned fitfully as he tried to rid his mind of the myriad things that kept him awake. He knew that these feelings would pass once the enquiry gained momentum and the path that should be taken became clearer but, right now, he needed sleep.

In the late afternoon, he phoned Collins and explained that he had submitted the forms to obtain Docherty's phone records and the conversation he had had with Neilson.

"He's hard work, isn't he?" Collins agreed when told.

"He certainly is, but, hopefully, he'll land himself in the shit with the bosses for not following the car lead."

"What about the images from the CCTV cameras?"

"Well, we got them blown up and managed to get them in colour, too. The pictures are still grainy and indistinct. Not enough that you can see his features, but they did manage to get him pictured against a low wall up by Old Dalkeith Road. That'll at least give us an idea of how tall he is. The coat he was wearing is green, by the way."

Stuart outlined where the wall was and described the male from the images. "He's about forty years old, thin or athletic build, with dark short hair. He's wearing this dark green Puffa-style jacket, black trousers, and boots. The case that he's carrying is also black, with rounded edges, not very thick, if you get my drift, and has brown or tan colouring at the carrying handle."

"I'm nightshift tonight, Willie. I'll take a drive up there and have a look at this wall that you're telling me about and see what size it is."

"It only comes up to about his waist and it's hard to say how far away from it he standing when the picture was taken. I'll be getting our boys to do that in the morning, anyway."

"It's the weekend tomorrow, mate."

"Maybe next week, then. I'm heading off home to introduce myself to the family again. Have a quiet weekend."

"I'll try, Willie, but you know what Fridays and Saturdays are like up the town -- five-pint hard men and barrack room lawyers everywhere. Still, keeps us in a job, eh?"

"I might be one of them. I need a blowout to try to get my head clear and stop thinking."

"Take care. I'll speak to you next week."

"Yeah. Cheers, Shug."

Stuart headed home and suggested to his wife that they go out for a meal in town, have a nice bottle of wine, and go on for a few drinks, to which she had readily agreed. He had a shower as his wife put on her makeup and looked out a pair of heels and a dress to match before heading for their favourite Italian restaurant.

After a few aperitifs, they enjoyed a relaxed evening eating and chatting, and slowly the thoughts on his mind passed into the background. After drinks in another few pubs, he was more than a few sheets to the wind, as was his wife, and, holding each other up, they made their way home.

As Stuart's head hit the pillow, a thought popped into his head, something that had always troubled him since it happened and always came back to him when he was pissed and under pressure. His mind wandered back to his early days as a young PC, when he had dealt with an assault and robbery in Edinburgh's city centre, where two young thugs had mugged a Canadian tourist for her handbag.

Unfortunately for them, she fought back valiantly and had been carrying a dog repellent pepper spray -- perfectly legal in Canada, but not so much here. As they attacked her, she sprayed both of them, with a devastating outcome. Stuart had never seen so much snot and tears, coughing and vomit, to say nothing of their bitching and whining.

Calling on the services of an old seasoned veteran of the CID, corroboration of the woman's story was provided by the fact that only the three of them had been affected, despite the thug's protestations of innocence, their nonsensical version of events, and the complaints that were registered against the officers.

It proved to be a very important lesson for Stuart, one that he had never forgotten: Criminals lie and cheat, as do witnesses on occasion, and so do lawyers, as the really hard time he endured during cross-examination in Court underlined for him. Why was the woman not charged with assault? Why she was not charged with possession of an offensive weapon? His two clients were fine upstanding members of the community, after all, although he subsequently found that they were related to gang activities.

He had answered the questions and was afforded a great deal of protection from a good PF and sympathetic sheriff, but from that point on, he vowed that he would get on the same level as the criminals. He would retain a reputation for playing the game fairly and squarely, but he would use their own tactics against them when the need arose. If he knew a man was guilty, that was good enough for him.

Stuart fell sound asleep, and he hardly moved all night, as evidenced by the single imprint of his head on the pillow, and the bed clothes hardly moved at all. He thereafter did nothing all weekend, apart from lounging about the house watching sport on TV, much to the annoyance of his wife, but, having been married to him for twenty-five years, she recognised and understood how he was feeling and gave him his space until he was ready to talk.

This was something that few people recognised or thought about when talking of police work and how it affected family life. The sights that many officers saw, the truly horrible crimes that they sometimes had to investigate, the cancelled rest days they were required to work, the hours they were kept on after their shift had been due to finish in order to complete an enquiry, their rest days spent sitting about in Court, or having to come back from annual leave for Court purposes. Julie Stuart had served her time just as long as her husband.

"Jules, can I ask you something?" Stuart finally asked on Sunday night.

"Surely."

"You know how I'm on another squad?"

"Yes, I know," she replied, sounding puzzled.

"We've got to try and find the killer, but we've got a real arsehole in charge. He doesn't want to lead, doesn't recognise good work, puts up barriers along the way, and has no real idea about what to do. But he's the boss. He might also be mixed up in other stuff, too…." He trailed off.

"You know what you're doing, Willie. God knows, you've done enough murder enquiries in your time. Do what your gut instinct tells you to do. It's been pretty much right all these years. We've all worked with idiots and had to play the political game and take it on the chin," she offered, remembering her time on the shop floor of a department store, when her efforts to make what she thought were attractive display layouts would be slated for no other reason than the manager didn't like it. No advice or direction was given regarding his or her opinions on how to make it better.

"Yeah, I know there will always be bosses, some better than others. But this guy is a tool, and there's a good chance that he's dishonest and mixed up in some big stuff."

"Well, in that case, Willie, go after him. If he's rotten, he needs caught. Keep your eye on the ball with the squad. It sounds like it'll almost run itself, anyway, but watch yourself. Don't let it get you down or affect your health. It's not worth that. It is just a job."

Just a job, Stuart repeated to himself. *It isn't personal. Just business.* He remembered the lines from the Godfather. *How appropriate,* he thought, smiling to himself.

At nine o'clock on Monday morning, he was back at his desk and felt more like himself. Almost as soon as he sat down, the phone was ringing.

"DI Stuart," he said into the handset.

"Willie, it's Dougie McInnes."

"Morning, Dougie," he said cheerfully. "How are you this morning?"

"No' very happy, if I'm honest," his superintendent answered.

"Oh, why?"

"I had Dick Neilson on the phone on Friday moaning about you, amongst other things."

"What have I done, like? Or not done, as the case may be?"

"Seems you're trying to take over the enquiry."

"I'm doing no such thing. Are you talking about the car that was seen up by The Wisp?"

"I am, that, yes. He said that you were undermining him and challenging his authority."

"We had a discussion at the back door of the station. I wanted to put the details of this car into the system, and he didn't. As far as I'm aware, it's not on it. You and I both know that it'll have to be investigated at the end of the day. I thought it deserved to be done sooner rather than later. He said no, and that was it."

"Well, that's not the version I got, but I said that I would have a word with you. I've done that, so now, how is the enquiry going?"

For the next several minutes, they talked about the progress that had been made, which consisted mainly of eliminating what people thought they had seen or heard, rather than the direction he thought that it should take in light of new leads.

"It'll all have to be done in any case, Dougie, but he's a hard man to work for or with. Why was he appointed?"

"Seems he's being groomed for greater things, Willie. It came from the top. They want him to have some squad experience for his CV. That's one of the reasons that I surrounded him with a good team. I know you guys can solve this, but he couldn't find his arse with both hands in the dark."

"Okay, thanks, Dougie. I appreciate your honesty. I'll mind my Ps & Qs."

Fucking rat, telling tales to teacher, he thought to himself as he hung up the phone.

Following another non-event of a briefing, the squad got back to work after their weekend. The tasking sheets were allocated, the teams went out to do as they had been instructed, and Stuart and Neilson returned to their offices to read through mounds of paper and on-screen documents.

It was mid-morning when he was given a list of registration numbers by his DS.

"There are quite a few, but I've highlighted the ones that the two uniformed cops did on that night. It just gives a list of the registration numbers on here, but the one that you'll be looking for is this one," he said, handing him a printout from PNC.

The registration number was clearly printed under the bright orange highlighter pen.

"And this is the one that doesn't have a current keeper?" he asked.

"Yup. That's it. There are a few details of previous keepers. It's an old car, but the previous owner should be able to tell us who they sold it to"

Stuart looked at the highlighted entry on the computer printout and saw that it was indeed an unregistered vehicle and that the previous owner was a Mrs Dorothy Neilson with an address at Riverside Gardens in Musselburgh, a town on the east side of Edinburgh.

"Can we get the guys looking at the CCTV to have a look for this car on the cameras, so that we can find out which way the car has come and gone from the locus? There might even be one of those ANPR cameras that pinged the registration?"

The Automatic Number Plate Recognition computer system had just recently been added to the Police armoury and the sited cameras could read thousands of car registration numbers on a daily basis. Any vehicle having no insurance or MOT or, as in this case, no registered keeper, would be highlighted to the traffic officers to follow up.

"You want someone to go round to the house and ask about the car?" the DS asked.

"No, not yet. I'll look after this aspect of the enquiry. The boss wants everything else looked at first."

"How far back do you want them to start looking?"

"I'd say start about six pm up to about nine pm. If there's nothing, add a couple of hours on each end and try again."

"Roger that, Willie," said the DS, and he was off about his duties again.

Rather than go straight to the address, Stuart knew it was best that he get himself up to speed with all the information about the car, the address, and this Mrs Dorothy Neilson. Forearmed is forewarned, after all. Firstly, he dialled up the address on the Force custody computer system to see if anyone had given the address when they had been arrested or detained, but without success. He then went to the station control room where the clerk of the office and the civilian assistant were busy answering calls on the telephone and enquiries at the front counter. When the clerk became free, he asked that the address be plumbed into the Command and Control system to see if the address had key holders for any alarm system that might be in operation. Again there was no success.

"What about the voters roll?" the clerk had suggested, and the name of the household that came back as resident at the address was not Neilson, but Cassiday. Next, he asked the clerk to input the vehicle registration number again and obtain a printout of the vehicle's previous owners and why it was unregistered. The clerk did as he was asked and deciphered the information on screen for him.

"It appears that this Mrs Neilson told DVLA that the vehicle was scrapped about three years ago. It shouldn't be on the road. There are no insurance details or MOT for it," he told him.

The Driver and Vehicle Licensing Authority kept records of every vehicle in the country, together with details of what insurance cover was held on the vehicle, who had taken out the policy, and who was entitled to drive the car, as well as details of the annual test certificate ensuring its roadworthiness. Stuart had hoped that Mrs Neilson's details would have been there. He knew that it was seldom that easy, but it was worth a try.

Thanking the clerk and taking his copy of the printout, he went back to his office and assumed his thinking position once more. After a few minutes, it came to him.

The Register of Sasines, he said to himself as he sat upright again.

The Sasines Register of Scotland maintained details of every house built in Scotland, current and previous owners, with details of mortgages provided in the case of privately owned houses.

They'll have details of the owners of the house, he said to himself.

He then phoned Register House and explained who he was and what he wanted. As it was part of the enquiry, there wouldn't be a problem with him obtaining the information and the required fees would not be applied.

"But all the information we have is online, if you want to have a look," he was told.
He thanked him and returned to his computer.

Logging into the Register of Scotland's website, he entered the details that he had and quickly learned that the property was indeed owned by Mrs Dorothy Neilson. At the foot of the page, there was a cross reference to an additional purchase that had been made twenty years after the original sale of the property had been recorded. It was for a garage or lock-up facility. He sat and digested the information.

He didn't know what the address looked like but came to the conclusion that it couldn't have a garage on the property, and it didn't look like it had been built as part of an extension. The details referred to a sale of a garage, but why was the owner of the property different from that of the occupier? Could it be rented out by Mrs Neilson? How would he find out without speaking to the occupier? Why were the names different?

Picking up the phone again, he contacted Edinburgh City Council and explained to the operator the reason for his phone call. "Musselburgh is not our area," he was told. "It'll be East Lothian Council that you're after."

He then dialled again and, once more, explained the information that he was after.

"I'll put you through to the housing benefit," the receptionist told him, and, shortly thereafter, he was speaking with an officer from the department. He gave the address and was put on hold whilst the information was gathered.

"Yes, there are claimants at that address," the official told him. "A James Cassiday is rented through a private landlord."

"Excellent," Stuart beamed. "I don't suppose you have details of the landlord?"

"We do, yes. A Richard Neilson with an address in Edinburgh. You want that?"

Willie wanted the address and almost dropped the phone when told.

Chapter Fifteen

    Ever since he had got into his first fight when he was at school, Dan Copeland knew that he could take care of himself. Always slightly larger than the other kids in his year, he got used to getting his own way and, as a consequence, frequently came into conflict with his teachers.

    As he grew older he was often subjected to corporal punishments for being disruptive in class or bullying others in the playground, and this he accepted as almost a badge of honour -- that his teachers could not change him or show him the error of his ways – and which made him well thought of in his small group of like-minded friends.

His parents, of course, worried about his behaviour and tried their best to keep him on the straight and narrow, but they were well aware that he always wanted to take the path of least resistance. He wasn't prepared to work hard at his studies and kept getting himself into trouble with the police. It was something that they hoped he would grow out of, but he didn't.

At sixteen years of age, after many years of having police officers calling at the house following his latest brush with the law, he was arrested and taken to the station for breaking into cars in the affluent Trinity area on the north side of Edinburgh, near to his Granton home. This time, it was different, however, as there was no need for the officers to contact his parents and have them attend at the station. He was now an adult and would be treated like one. On more than one occasion, had been beaten up in the cell after refusing to admit his guilt.

The more he was arrested, the more fines he had to pay at Court, and the more he had to go out at night stealing in order to fund his lifestyle. Stolen cars would be driven around all night, sometimes others would be stolen from different parts of the city, or broken into for the valuables that had been left on open display. He had an extensive criminal record by the time he was twenty, and the Courts were left with no other recourse than a prison sentence. Again, this had no effect on him, and he learned the ins and outs of the legal and penal systems from his fellow inmates.

Whilst inside jail, with his aversion to reading, he used the sporting facilities often and trained hard with the gym monsters who lifted weights. Other inmates didn't mess with these guys due to their outright physical ability to beat the shit out of anyone who incurred their wrath and, upon release, he continued his training.

Dissatisfied with the speed of his progress, he resorted to steroids and very quickly the dianabol that he pumped into his system every week began to give him the growth that he sought. Very soon, he required gyms with larger and larger stacks of weights able to accommodate his growing physique.

As time passed, he was no longer talked about in derogatory terms by others, certainly not within his earshot, and he was able to start his own small-scale trade in drugs via his steroid supplier. Following a particularly profitable night's housebreaking where he and a friend stole a sizeable amount of cash and jewellery, he "invested" the money, buying a larger than normal amount of drugs – cannabis, to begin with and progressing to "speed" (amphetamine),"snow" (cocaine), "smack" (heroin), and "ecstasy" (MDMA). This brought him to the attention of other suppliers in the area and, whilst in his local pub one evening, he was approached by two local enforcers and warned to stop trading.

"This is a friendly warning," they said as they left the pub.

Copeland followed them outside as they walked to their car. Picking up a half brick from the roadside, Copeland ran after them. As the first one turned to see who was following them, he brought the brick down on his head with a sickening blow, splitting his skull open, immediately rendering the man senseless, blood pumping from the wound inflicted.

Copeland followed up the attack by viciously punching the second man square in the face with his huge fist, sending him reeling backwards, his upper lip split completely through, so that it parted in the middle. He continued to punch and kick him as he bent forwards in pain until he fell to the ground in very obvious submission. But this had no effect on Copeland as he rained down blows upon his semi-conscious victim.

"Don't you fucking ever come into a pub and threaten me. You hear me? You fucking hear me?" He accepted the nod that he was given as a "yes."

Returning to the pub, he demanded and was given the copy of the tape from the pub's CCTV system monitoring the car park. They knew him well enough to refuse.

And slowly, but nevertheless surely, he had progressed through the hierarchy of the drugs trade, diversifying his money into cash businesses, such as the taxi trade, car washes, and strip joints in order to hide his assets. He was a wealthy man by his mid-twenties, with a formidable reputation in the north side of the city, and he was looking to expand his business interests southwards, following Buchan's murder.

But, as he walked out the gym at Newcraighall on a crisp, bright winter morning, all that came to an end as a sniper's bullet ripped into his chest, shattering the car windscreen behind him as the bullet passed through his body, hurling him backwards onto the bonnet where his heels rattled against a headlight for a few seconds. A second bullet took off the back of his head as he lay propped up against the roof of the car, and then he was still.

"Aw, for fuck's sake!" was all that Willie Stuart could muster when he was told about the second shooting. "Who is it?"

"Danny Copeland, at a gym in Newcraighall. Another high power rifle, apparently," his DS told him.

"Well, we canny get involved with it right now. If it's connected with our enquiry, the bosses will let us know in due course. We need to concentrate on what we're doing. How are you getting on with finding the green Fiesta on the CCTV cameras, by the way?"

"Nothing yet. I've got the videos in for Old Dalkeith Road out towards the bypass, the videos for Newcraighall Road out to the bypass, but only a couple of guys to sit and watch it."

"You might have less than that by tomorrow, at this rate," Stuart suggested, knowing that a second squad would have to be set up, offices found, and resources put in place to work on that case. "What's our boss got to say? I'm assuming you've told him already?"

"No, I haven't seen him at all today. I don't think he's in. He must be at a meeting somewhere."

"Okay, then. Feed the information about the Fiesta into the HOLMES system. Let's generate some official enquiries along those lines. Get the good images that we have of the guy carrying the case out to the cops on the street. We're looking for suggestions as to who he is."

"I thought that the boss didn't want that stuff put in for action?" his DS asked.

"Well, he's not here right now so I guess it's up to me to make the decision. If I get a hard time, it'll not be the first bollocking I've had."

"I hope to Christ that this isn't the start of the retaliation from Buchan's lot," the DS said. "That'll surely shoot holes in the senior officer's so-called war on drugs they keep banging on about."

The various operations that were becoming the norm, with their usual media sound bites attached regarding the "Slaying of the dragon," or it being an "intelligence lead operation," that the "communities wouldn't tolerate it." Whilst there had been successes, with some excellent recoveries, most cops knew that there would be plenty of people only too willing to step into the vacancy left by the dealers who had been jailed. Most cops grew to be cynical, some more so than others. It came with the territory as, every single day, people lied to them.

"I hope not. I really do. I remember the last time this happened and it wasn't pretty," Stuart said, but underneath, deep down, he knew that it had been coming. Where about, he hadn't known. But he knew that it would happen.

"I'd better phone the super and see if this is going to change us at all."

"Okay, Willie. I'll leave you to it."

Stuart picked up the phone and called his boss at Force HQ.

"Superintendent McInnes," he said, deadpan into the phone

"Hello, boss. It's Willie Stuart, sorry to bother you. I know you'll be busy."

"You don't know the half of it," came his laconic reply. "You'll have heard about the second shooting, I'm assuming," McInnes asked.

"I have, yes. You'll be getting another squad organised. So apologies for adding to your list. I need to speak to you."

"Oh. What about?"

"About our squad and where it's going. Dick Neilson wasn't in today and nobody has seen him. Are you aware?"

"No, I wasn't. Is he off sick?"

"Maybe, but I haven't checked. I've been doing a fair bit of enquiries into Buchan and other things that I think you should know, but I think that I should speak to you in person. There's another cop that's been helping me, but I think the time has come to get outside help."

"What do you mean? Outside help?" McInnes quizzed him.

"Can I come down to see you tomorrow?"

"I think you'd better, Willie. I think you'd better."

Stuart hung up the phone and then called Collins on his mobile.

"Hey there, Shug. It's Willie. Are you working or days off?"

"Days off. Just finished nightshift. Why?"

"You and I are going to see Super McInnes tomorrow and we're going to put our cards on the table."

"What for?"

"There's been another shooting of a drugs main man today. Dan Copeland, from the north side, has had the back of his head blown off. Early days yet, but I think that both Buchan and him getting killed will be connected. Maybe it's retaliation for Buchan, maybe not. I don't know, but the squads will have to share information if they are at all connected. It's too big a fish to lose whilst were playing it," he said, hoping Collins would appreciate the fishing analogy.

"Well, if you're sure, Willie," Collins said with a fair degree of scepticism in his voice, "if you're sure."

Chapter Sixteen

Stuart and Collins arrived at Police HQ early the following morning. Despite him being on a day off, Collins came in for the meeting that they were about to have with McInnes, knowing that he would claim back the time at a later date, or, if he was lucky, he could claim the overtime. He'd been instructed to come in by a Detective Inspector after all. They bumped into each other in the canteen where each was buying a coffee and a "pig bun" or bacon roll.

"Shall we just go up and see him now?" Collins suggested.

"We'd better give him half an hour or so to get his conference calls done and dusted first. He'll be a busy man this morning," he said, knowing that, in addition to updating all the senior officers about developments that had occurred overnight concerning the murder of Daniel Copeland, there was all of the day-to-day business to be accounted for, too.

After finishing their rolls and coffee, they slowly walked up to the second floor where McInnes' office was situated and knocked on his open door. He looked up and signalled with his fingers to give him two minutes, almost like Winston Churchill.

"He needs two minutes. Either that, or he's telling us to fuck off," Stuart said to Collins, laughing.

"Well at least you're at ease with this, Willie. If I'm honest, I'm almost shitting myself."

"What for? We've got nothing to hide. We've not done anything wrong; just bent the rules a little and everything that we have and have done was for very good reasons. Besides, Dougie and

I go back a long way. He's one of the good guys." Stuart and McInnes had joined the service on the same intake and had gone to the Police College together. Their careers had crossed paths many times, with McInnes gaining his promotions in a similar vein to Stuart, although more rapidly and more often.

"I never like speaking to bosses at his rank. I'm always wondering what they're thinking and what they're likely to do or say," Collins offered.

"We'll be fine, Shug," came Stuart's confident reply.

"Okay, Willie, in you come," Dougie McInnes boomed as he shouted to them outside in the corridor. He was from the old school and didn't stand on ceremony.

Nearing the end of his service, although as a senior officer he could stay on if he wished, he had seen a lot of change and had dismissed much of it as crap. He would, of course, never admit to that. He could speak knowledgeably about integrated strategies or pathway projects and other such terminologies, but deep down all he wanted was for cops to go out on the street, catch the bad guys, and lock them up.

"Take a seat, gents," McInnes said and waved his hands at the chairs in the corner of the office.

"Thanks," Stuart said, closing the door behind them. "This is Hugh Collins, one of the firearms guys in the ARV unit. He's been helping me on our enquiry." Collins nodded at McInnes in response to his introduction.

"Right, then," Stuart continued. "Where to start?" He paused to gather his thoughts.

McInnes gave nothing away as he looked at the both of them.

"When Buchan got shot, I was a bit surprised that Dick Neilson was appointed SIO, never having done anything like a murder enquiry before. From the start, he seems to have been putting up barriers in our way when we wanted to advance the enquiry. Following our little chat the other day about me undermining him, I gave it a lot of thought."

"Go on," McInnes said.

"We've done the standard enquiries to date, following up what witnesses say they saw and have been chasing ghosts, if I'm honest. It's got to be done, I know, but when we got a good lead with the images of the man in black and then the Fiesta car that was parked up near the locus, Neilson stopped us from putting it into the system. That was the reason for our conversation the other day."

"What Fiesta?" McInnes asked, looking confused.

"There was an old green Fiesta parked up at the Wisp on the night in question. Two cops checked it out but were called away. When they came back to the car, it was gone. We traced it back through the cops' PNC enquiry and got the registration number. It's unregistered but was previously owned by a Mrs Dorothy Neilson, with an address in Musselburgh. I think it's Dick Neilson's mother's car."

"Okay," McInnes said slowly.

"The address that it was registered to in Musselburgh has tenants living in it. Some folks called Cassiday. We haven't been to the address yet and we're looking at CCTV to try and trace the movements of the car. Shug, here, had done a good bit of enquiry," Stuart nodded in Collins direction, "and found out that Neilson was at a deer shoot down in the Borders a good while back, and it appears that Neilson gave a guy called Harry King a run home after he got pished at the shoot. Harry owned a Blaser .308 that folded down into a small, hard-shell carrying case. It seems that Harry was a bit of a piss head and he was plastered on the day and passed out when he got home. He woke up to find his rifle stolen and a window smashed. He reported it as an HB."

"Okay. I'm with you so far," McInnes offered.

"There was a fingerprint found at the locus, on a glass pick out. It was examined but no match came back and it's still unidentified. I think it could be Neilson's, but as we don't routinely search police fingerprints we needed a DCIs authority to have it done."

"And?"

"Neilson was the DCI in Professional Standards at the time of the HB. Any application to search through cops' prints, he would know about. He could block the application easily. And that brings me to our other problem." McInnes was sitting back in his chair listening intently, giving nothing away as Stuart related his story.

"Shug, here," he continued, nodding his head at Collins again, "was on the drugs searches following Buchan murder. He turned up a notebook at Ryan Docherty's house, written in Morse code, of all things."

"Morse code?" McInnes said, almost shouting.

"Yeah, he used to be in the Navy before he got kicked out for peddling Jamaican woodbines, instead of navy shag." Everyone in the room got the reference to marijuana and smiled. "But the notebook had Neilson's name in it with details of money, which we think he was getting from Buchan. Shug's still got it, but we thought it best to keep it away from the proper channels because of what happened next."

"For fuck's sake. What happened next, then? McInnes said, sounding impatient but not meaning to be.

"I know, I know. But I was contacted by someone outside the force telling me that Neilson was blocking intelligence reports about Buchan getting put into the database. Seems he was using a couple of LIOs to help him. We don't know why yet. Shug, here, stumbled over it, too, after he put in a couple of entries but couldn't find them later when he went back to check. He reported the matter to Professional Standards but was knocked back and nothing seems to have been done. The two LIOs were moved out of their positions and the information started flowing again."

"But you said the two LIOs were moved?" McInnes questioned.

"True, but it doesn't appear that they were disciplined for anything. Just moved out of their positions. I don't think that they know why they were moved. Anyway, we checked back through Docherty's phone SIM card."

"You've got his fucking SIM card, too?" McInnes gasped.

"Yes, we have. We plugged it into another phone and checked back on the calls received from other phones, and we think we found the phone number Buchan used to contact Docherty. He was used as the bag man who dropped off money for Neilson."

"How do you know that?"

"Docherty told me after I leaned on him a bit, telling him he'd be in deep shit if it got out that we had his phone and notations."

"Jesus, Willie. You're sailing mighty close to the wind."

"Again, I know, but for very good operational reasons. If Neilson is dirty, and I think he is, we had to keep all the information away from him. That, and we didn't know who else was involved or how high up the chain this went."

"So, then, what do you need from me, then? Why are you telling me this now?" McInnes asked.

"Because we could carry on as we've been going, but that would be pretty much illegal. We need to access phone records, police fingerprint records, apply for warrants to search houses, and get official information from the guy outside the force who told me about the intelligence records. There's obviously firearms involved. We can't go after anyone officially, knowing that we could be putting them in real danger of getting shot."

"You mean accessing a guy's phone without the written authority is not illegal?"

"I would say that it was not standard operating procedure, rather than illegal," Stuart responded. "Semantics, maybe, but open to interpretation."

"Who else knows about this?" McInnes asked.

"Not very many. Shug and I know them and have worked with them before. But you'll have to appreciate that I won't tell you who they are. If someone is going to get into the shit about this, I'll carry that can alone."

"Very big and brave of you, Willie. The end justifies the means and all that noble minded horseshit?"

"Something like that, Boss," Stuart almost sounded contrite and started wondering if he had indeed gone too far and was now for the high jump.

"Okay, then, Willie. You've put your cards on the table. Let me be frank," Stuart and Collins glanced at each other fleetingly, with Collins returning Stuart's glance with an *I told you so* look.

"You're right," McInnes said bluntly. "You're right in what you say. The guy you spoke with outside the force is Davie

Leadbetter; right?" Stuart was taken aback but tried not to show it. *How the hell did he know that?*

He continued. "I was given the heads-up by Davie Leadbetter a wee while back about Neilson. The guy that the Scottish Crime Squad had on the inside of Buchan's OCG was very good." McInnes began, using the acronym that was in vogue. An Organised Crime Group was a criminal gang.

"He got wind of the fact that Neilson was on the payroll and has been stealing from Buchan. He's been taking money out of the country for him but not putting it all where he should have. The intelligence entries, I know about, too, but only the Chief Super and I know about them. It was me who had the LIOs moved without getting fixed for anything. Then we had Buchan's murder -- and it really was -- decided on-high that he should be moved. He'd been applying for transfers out of Professional Standards, anyway. Why, I don't know. You don't apply to get into the CID at Chief Inspector rank. You're appointed."

"For fuck's sake, Dougie!" Stuart had now dropped any formality with his boss. Collins shifted uncomfortably in his chair.

"Like I said to you at the time, Willie, I surrounded Neilson with a good team that I knew would do the business for me and the Force. I didn't know how far Buchan's tentacles reached into the Force, either, or who else was involved. But I know you from way back and know that you're the man to get me a result and would do a good job."

"So it was a test. A fucking integrity test?"

"I wouldn't say that, Willie. Not in those words. It was an avenue to explore where we could go to get information, solid information that we could use to bring down Buchan and get Neilson at the same time for his corruption in office. Right now, we have this notebook, the SIM card, and the two LIOs. We should get Buchan's mobile phone records soon and use it to trace other phone numbers and individuals involved. Like I said earlier, the ends justifies the means."

"Et tu, Brute?" Stuart replied laconically.

"Indeed," McInnes replied in similar tones, with a smile. Knowing Stuart's liking for Shakespeare, "All's fair in love and war," he continued.

Stuart looked over at Collins, saying, "See, I told you everything would be alright on the night."

"So, Willie, who else is involved? I need to know," McInnes asked in serious tones.

"Well, there's us, John Reynolds from the drugs squad who was there when Shug found the notebook, my DS who's been doing stuff off the radar, Jimmy Wilkinson."

"And my partner, Jamie Beattie," Collins chipped in. "It was him and I who found the notebook and SIM card in Docherty's house. We work together on the ARV."

"Okay, then," McInnes said. "The Chief has given me complete authority on this one. I stress here and now that this must stay on the QT. Nobody can know anything about what I'm about to say. Do you understand?" Stuart and Collins could see that his tone had changed and he was now deadly serious. "I want the five of you to take this enquiry to a logical conclusion. Solve the murder and if it's linked to the latest Copeland murder, solve that, too. I'll make sure that you get updates from the squad that's been set up to investigate that one. Find out what Neilson has been up to, how much money he's managed to squirrel away, where it is, and get it back. Buchan's dead, but he's still not getting to keep his money. Neither is Neilson. Nail his arse to a door, Willie."

"Is that all?" Stuart asked, half in jest.

"No, that's not all of it. I'll make arrangements for your firearms boys," he said, looking at Collins, "to get a standing authorisation to carry weapons when you're doing the enquiry. Health and safety and a bit of contingency planning," he carried on with a wry grin on his face. "Any enquiries that you need authority for, come through me. Good, old fashioned detective work please, Willie. No pre-signed warrants that you might have stashed away in your bottom drawer," a further reference to a habit old-school detectives had had in years gone by, of having a Justice of the Peace sign a couple of warrants for future use. Something that they had been only too happy to oblige with.

"Oh, for the good old days," Stuart echoed his boss's sentiments.

"This needs to be able to stand up in Court, Willie. What's more, it has to be seen to stand up. The damage to the Force's reputation is very real," McInnes cautioned them both, looking from one to the other and back again.

"Carry on as you are right now. I'll get you an office here so that I can expedite any forms you may have. And of course keep an eye on you! You'll have to stay on the Buchan enquiry for now, Willie, until we find out what's happened to Neilson. He's not turned up again; nor phoned in sick. Nobody knows where he is."

Chapter Seventeen

As had happened with the Buchan enquiry, and the many times before that, the police response to Copeland's murder kicked into gear. A helpful difference this time was that it had occurred during the day when most resources were already available, and duty, which allowed for a quicker response from all concerned.

After the preliminary work had been completed, a search team was brought in to examine the locus. The POLSA leading the search was armed with aerial photographs from Google maps which showed that the gym was surrounded by a bypass motorway, a slip road on one side, and a railway line to the rear. There was a large patch of waste ground at the rear of a wooded area running parallel to the railway line that gave access to another car parking area in front of a small shopping complex. On the other side of the railway line, heading east, was a large housing estate with a footbridge that gave the residents access to the shops.

Whilst Stuart and Collins were having their discussion with McInnes, the search teams had got to work in the woods. First, they had had a walkthrough of the area, setting their search parameters with police incident tape attached to the trees, and this was followed by a fingertip search of the smaller sections now plainly separated. When that proved to be negative, each section had its undergrowth cut back, the contents being bagged and sifted through to ensure nothing was missed. There was obviously a lot of litter that had been deposited within the woods, or having been blown there by the wind, trapped by the trees.

However, the search teams did their work assiduously, and eventually they turned up an empty shell casing, obviously discernible by its bright, shiny look, lying about ten metres into the wood next to the railway fencing and in a position that gave a clear line of sight down one of the rows of planted trees over towards the car park of the gym.

Forensically recovered, it had been sent for full examination. They had been very lucky to have found it so early, but each member of the team knew that they would have to continue through the whole of the woods looking for anything else that might prove to have evidential value, just to be sure.

After their meeting, Stuart and Collins had left McInnes' office somewhat dumbfounded but definitely relieved. Although Stuart would not admit to it, he had had feelings of trepidation about telling his boss what he had -- what they had -- been up to.

"McInnes is a good boss, Shug. He knows the ropes and he should get most of what he said he would up and running PDQ," Stuart said to his shell-shocked partner in crime.

"How soon is pretty damn quick, then?" Collins asked.

"He'll have you guys seconded to this mini-squad today. Expect a phone call later today from your admin. I'll go and speak to John Reynolds now, and I'll speak to Jimmy Wilks later when I get back to Craigmillar. It'll be soon though. There really isn't much time to waste. I'll see if the other guys can come down for a meeting tonight about six pm."

And, true to his word, Collins did get a phone call later telling him that he and Jamie Beattie were being removed from shifts on the ARV for a special detail. As he hung up the phone, Beattie was on the line to him.

"Special detail? What's this all about, Shug?"

"I can't say right now, mate, but are you free tonight about six pm?"

"I can be," he responded, "but I'm a bit wary of sticking my head above the parapet and volunteering for something that I know nothing about."

"Trust me, Jamie," Collins replied. "I was like that this morning, too."

Later that night, after the Buchan squad had packed for the night and all the staff had gone home, the mini-squad gathered. Stuart introduced everyone, and they all nodded to each other or shook hands, none of them sure why they were there or the nature of the work they were expected to do.

"Let me explain, gentlemen," Stuart said, and then ran through his conversation with McInnes, what had been discovered to date, his suspicions, and the nature of the enquiry that they were about to undertake. When he had finished, Beattie, Reynolds, and Wilkinson all sat back in their chairs and, almost in unison, let out expletives.

"Yeah, I know," Collins said, breaking the silence.

"Operation Iago is what I think we'll call ourselves. It won't appear on any paperwork. Don't refer to it by name and, above all, *DO NOT* speak to anyone outside this group about what we are doing," Stuart said, reinforcing his earlier points. "If any bosses ask you what you're doing, just refer them to Mr McInnes and keep schtum."

"Iago?" Reynolds asked.

"You know? The bad guy from Othello. The one about jealousy, revenge, and betrayal. I thought it was quite appropriate. Anyway, first things first. Until we get Buchan's phone records back, we're going to press on with following up the car lead, the images of the man in black, and we'll need to get that fingerprint from the HB in Hawick, the Harry King break-in, identified. I'll do that with Wilks," he glanced at his DS. "We're here anyway, Jim."

Wilks nodded in agreement. "John," he continued, "I want you to get the SIM card and the notebook and go through it together with Shug and Jamie. Double check everything and make sure nothing is missed. When you get Buchan's phone records, do a comparison and try write it up in a form that is easily read and can be cross-referenced for Court. Chase up any of the numbers that are on both phones, and see if you can get them identified."

All three of them nodded their agreement

"And while you're at it, try get a hold of Neilson's passport number. HM Border Force will be able to help you with that. We need to find out where he's been going if he's carrying money out the country for Buchan and, of course, how he's been doing it."

"Roger that, Willie," Collins said. "What about the standing authorisation McInnes was talking about?"

"Well, as you know, that'll have to go up the executive for them to make a decision. Come in tomorrow in jeans, or whatever, and we'll see what happens. You'll be able to get a hold of covert holsters?" Stuart asked, not sure if they would be able to obtain the small leather strap that clipped onto a belt, higher up and out of sight under a jacket.

"Well, the chief instructor probably won't be happy about that. But then he never is, anyway. They're really meant for the protection guys, but I suppose we'll be protecting you guys," Collins replied.

"All sorted, then. Any questions?" he asked the assembled group. There were none. "Exchange all of your mobile numbers. We won't be using radios."

The following morning, all the members of Operation Iago began their respective tasks with a new found enthusiasm. Collins, Beattie, and Reynolds found a quiet corner of the force HQ building with computer facilities and began the laborious job of writing all the information on to a spreadsheet with dates and times calls were made or received, who from or who to, and any values were appended in the margins. Most of it was a straight copy of what Collins had already written down from the details in the notebook. It was mid-morning when Stuart phoned Collins mobile telling him that he had been sent Buchan's phone records.

"I'll email it to you. Good hunting," was all he said and all three knew that it was going to take a while. Time was something that they might not have, so they tried to work as quickly and as efficiently as possible. Fortunately, due to Buchan doing most of his dealings face-to-face and not writing anything down that could be used against him, there were only five numbers in his phone records. As they had suspected, though, there was no contract for the phone, so there weren't any details of the phone's owner.

"That'll make our job just that wee bit easier, then. We won't have to be applying for too many more records," Reynolds suggested.

The first enquiry they did was checking all the numbers from Buchan's phone against those held on record in Force custody computer. Anyone who had been arrested had the right to have a lawyer and one other reasonably named person informed of his or her arrest. This information was always input along with the name of the person being contacted. They might have been lucky, but they weren't.

Next, they tried SID, the Scottish Intelligence Database, and they managed to identify two numbers as associates of Buchan. Of course, whether they still had the same phones was a different matter, but by cross-referencing the dates the calls were made from Buchan's phone with the dates Neilson had supposedly received money, they narrowed the field considerably until they were happy that they knew, or at least strongly suspected, that they had it right.

Reynolds typed up a phone records data protection request and emailed it to McInnes' personal address within the Force. They already knew the number of Docherty's phone and that only left the last two numbers.

"Why don't we just phone them?" Beattie suggested. "If we use a landline from here, it'll come up as a blocked caller so whoever answers won't know it's us. They might not answer it, right enough."

"Willie wants us to have hard evidence, though," Reynolds cautioned.

"Aye, but we'll submit forms for these numbers and have to wait for the records to come back. We could get ahead of the game."

They looked at each other, obviously unsure.

"Could be worth a try? It's not Neilson's phone, we know that, I think." Collins offered.

Reynolds picked up a landline handset and dialled the first number. It rang for what seemed like minutes to Collins, with Beattie hunched over his shoulders. An answering machine kicked in as they listened to the message.

Hi. This is Bill Whyte. I can't come to the phone right now. Leave a message. Reynolds didn't, and hung up immediately.

"Silly boy!" he said. "Matty wouldn't be happy if he were alive."

Beattie was already at the computer terminal searching through records for Bill Whyte, trying every permutation of Bill and William with variations of spelling Whyte or White. There was no record that they could find, however.

"Try the other number," Collins suggested.

Reynold dialled it but the number was now unobtainable. "Alright, then. We need to find out who this Bill Whyte is. I'm open to suggestions," he said, sitting back in his chair.

The other two members of Iago team were equally busy that day. Stuart and Wilks had visited the fingerprint department where the paper records of police elimination prints were retained. Cops new to the job always had their fingerprints taken and input on a computer database nowadays, but when Neilson had joined, it was paper records only.

The fingerprint department was very busy following the latest shooting of Copeland, but they managed to speak with a DS, asking if he could search the records for an old break-in that had occurred in Hawick a few years back. Their request that it should be compared against police fingerprints elicited a quizzical glance from the DS.

"It's just for elimination, of course. There was a rifle stolen, same calibre as the one that killed Matty Buchan. It's just routine" Stuart had lied

"Okay. Gimme a minute," the DS sighed, as he got up and raked through various files of unidentified fingerprints until he found the photograph of the print he was looking for.

"Who's the cop?"

Stuart didn't give Neilson's name, just his collar number, and the DS busied himself again for the next several minutes.

Taking both records to a monitor that would enlarge both images to allow them to be compared on a split screen, he sat for several minutes tracing lines, ridges, and islands, counting in from the sides, top, and bottom and then placing dots on the left side of the monitor. He then sat back

"I'd say it's his. I've stopped at sixteen points. That's good enough for me," he said.

"Could you get it double-checked? Sorry about this. I know you're busy, but it's important," Stuart apologised.

"Dawn!" he shouted over his shoulder. "Could you double-check this for me, please?"

Dawn stopped what she was doing, as the DS wiped the left-hand screen clear, and then, taking the seat, she began the process again. After a few minutes, she declared, "Yes. I agree. That's him."

"Great," Stuart said. "One last thing. Could you write it up and send it to me personally?" he asked, knowing that he might be thought to be taking the piss.

"I'll add it to my 'to do' list," the DS replied, deadpan.

"Good enough," Stuart said. "I appreciate your helping us at short notice. While I'm here," he looked to see the DS rolling his eyes heavenwards, "I heard that they'd recovered a shell casing from the Copeland locus. Any joy with that?"

"A partial print, I think. Not much there, but we'll see what we can do."

"Thanks again," Stuart said, knowing that he'd pushed as far as he should go.

Chapter Eighteen

Enoch "Knuckles" McNally sat alone in his cell, running the events that had led to his arrest through his head for the umpteenth time. It had been a reasonably quiet night for him and his fellow doormen until a group of lads, obviously celebrating the result of a football match, had arrived at their club seeking admission.

As it was a quiet night, some of them had been allowed entry on the understanding that no scarves could be worn. Some had agreed, with some refusing to put away their team colours, and they had been turned away as a result. It was obvious that some had had too much to drink. As invariably happened in these circumstances, those who had been refused began to argue with the door staff, demanding the reason for their being refused.

Most of the time, the lads accepted the door staff decisions with a few well-aimed epithets concerning the marriage status of the doormen's parents, and could be persuaded to go on their way when reinforcements were called up from within the nightclub. Not this night however, when a large-scale brawl had flared up. Individual fights ensued as the doormen were attacked by two, three, or four supporters at once, like a pack of feral dogs, or were targeted if they were seen to be in a position of disadvantage.

It was in these type of scenarios that Knuckles came into his own and where he used his six-feet-six-inch, twenty-stone frame to devastating effect. Drawing a Taser from inside his jacket pocket, something that he had bought and illegally imported a few years ago from the United States, he zapped the person in front of him with a five-second burst, causing him to drop like a stone in front of him, as the high voltage surged through his body.

Knuckles was unconcerned that others who were in contact with his victim also felt the Tasers effects. Incensed that one of their number had been felled, he was attacked from all sides. Whilst the other doormen retreated to the main entrance to prevent any gaining access to the nightclub, Knuckles began to wage war on his own, swatting away half-hearted drunken punches, landing several telling blows, confident in his ability and sobriety.

He was not the kind of person to advance then retreat after landing a good punch, but rather stood his ground like the trained fighter he was. Not that he was fighting by the rules of the Marquis of Queensberry. Neither were his opponents, as he was struck a terrific blow to the back of his head with a large parking cone. Stunned briefly, he remained on his feet as the supporters swarmed over him as he paused to regain his senses. Knuckles was kicked and punched to his head and body continuously for several minutes until his colleagues came to assist him, allowing him a moment of respite.

As his head cleared, the red mist descended, and he sought out his assailant, exacting a terrible revenge, knocking him down with a devastating punch and following up with full-force kicks and stamps to his head. The other supporters backed off, wary of having the same treatment meted out upon themselves.

That was what the police had seen as they arrived, in response to the unfolding events which had been monitored by the City in View CCTV operator, who had contacted them by radio. Knuckles had, of course, protested his innocence – he was acting in self-defence, after all -- but the CCTV, the fractured skull and broken jaw inflicted on the target of his wrath told a different story.

Knuckles had been arrested and detained pending his appearance at Court the next lawful day, after giving a "No Comment" interview with the local CID officers who had been brought in to deal with the incident due to the severity of injury involved. His illegally held Taser was also damning him as, despite what he had been told to the contrary, it was classed as a firearm, and he knew that he was looking at time inside courtesy of Her Majesty.

He has been arrested many times before, of course, but not for a few years, as his boss, Matty Buchan, always wanted to keep a low profile and, although he had enforced Buchan's wishes on many people, many times before, it was always below the radar of the harsh light of publicity. He knew Matty would not have been happy with him, were he alive, and that he would have had some explaining to do to assuage his anger at the problems he had caused. But Matty wasn't in charge anymore, and he had been thinking about moving up in the world. That would have to wait until his present predicament resolved itself, one way or another.

Knuckles had no idea what time it was when he heard the sound of the key turning in the lock of his cell door. Looking up, he saw an old associate walk in.

"Hello, Knuckles," Willie Stuart said as he entered with Jim Wilkinson, offering his hand.

"Hello there, Mr Stuart," he said, taking the offered hand and shaking it in his bear-like paw.

"What have you been up to now?"

"Oh, you know how it is. You know me, too," he replied, now on his guard as to what he would say. He had been visited before by police when he had been locked up and knew that they always wanted something from him.

"Aye, I do, Knuckles. You and me go back a long way," Stuart said, turning to Wilkinson. "He was my first good arrest. What were you, eighteen?" he asked, returning his gaze to Knuckles.

"Aye, something like that."

"I think it was me who gave you your name; wasn't it?"

"Aye," Knuckles said.

"He was one of the first guys I came across to have the four dots tattooed on the knuckles of his right hand. *All Police Are Bastards*, it means. But it was appropriate given your first name and the nature of your work," Stuart said over his shoulder to his colleague.

"So, are you involved in my case then, Mr Stuart?" he asked.

"No, not me. We've got the job of trying to find out who killed Matty."

"I hope you find them, then. He was a good friend of mine."

"Yes, I know. You and Matty go back a long way, too. And that's what I wanted to ask you. Do you have anything that might help us?"

"I can't help you, Mr Stuart. Even though Matty's dead, you know I can't help you."

"I know that, Knuckles, but you need to help yourself with this one. The boy you done over is on life support, mate. It'll be attempted murder or assault to the endangerment of life at the very least. Then you've got to add in the Taser that you had. They're classed as firearms, here. That's a big one, too."

Despite what he had said to Stuart, Knuckles knew that he was in deep shit and that if he had any ideas of taking over some or all of Matty's business interests, he would have to act quickly. Something that he could not do if he was in jail or remanded in custody. Knuckles knew that Stuart knew that, too; hence, his visit.

"Listen, mate," Stuart continued, "I know you as a pretty straight bloke. I disagree with what you've done in the past, and you know me as someone who plays a straight game, as well. You and I both know that you'll never get your hands on Matty's money. He's got it planked away somewhere pretty much untouchable. You'll only be able to take over some of his businesses and start from scratch. I'm only interested in getting Matty's killer. If it's someone from your side, they'll be out of the picture. If it's the opposition, they'll be out of the picture, too," Stuart said, playing the same hand of cards that had worked with Ryan Docherty.

"What can you offer me, then?" Knuckles asked.

"I can't get you out of this one. You know that. But what I can do is have a word with the PF and let him know that you've helped us with our enquiry. I'm not looking for you to be an informer. I know you're not that kind of guy."

"I don't know, Mr Stuart. I don't know."

Stuart could sense in him a desire to make his situation easier. Knuckles was a big tough hombre, he knew, but self-preservation was a great lever to exert on him. All he needed was another nudge.

"A few guys have been giving us little bits of information already. The game's started for what Matty's left behind, and everyone's looking for a kick of the ball."

"Who?" Knuckles asked, with almost child-like innocence.

"Well, I'm not going to tell you who, but I'm not lying, mate. I've been through this type of thing once before, as have you, although you were just a youngster," Stuart said to him, referring to twenty years before when he had arrested Knuckles for a serious assault after he had kicked the shit out of a rival during Buchan's rise to the top of the pile.

That got Knuckles thinking again, difficult as he found it, having been awake most of the night.

"It's dog-eat-dog out there right now. We already know about the cop that was in Matty's pocket," Stuart said nonchalantly.

That one took Knuckles completely by surprise, and Stuart saw the surprised look on his face. *Maybe he didn't know after all?* he thought.

"I've no idea who that is, though. I can't help you."

"I don't need your help on that. We know who he is," Stuart repeated. "Like I said before, you ain't gonna take over Matty's business without a fight. Maybe I take away a piece of the puzzle for you? If you don't know anything, fine. I'll leave it there."

"I don't know who killed Matty, though. There's loads of folks who wanted him out of the picture."

"Listen, you did jobs for Matty. We know that. We know most of the guys on Matty's side of the city. It's the ones we don't know about that might hold the key," Stuart interrupted. "Someone after his money, stealing his money, or had crossed him in some way. What would you be giving up? Nothing to you. Matty's dead and his money's gone, too. You think that they're going to deal with you just like Matty? There's going to be a whole new game in town, Knuckles."

"The only boy I know like that is the boy Whyte. I dropped off money to him for Matty now and again."

Stuart looked over at Wilkinson briefly and then back at Knuckles. The obvious question was who was he, and how much had he dropped off to him, but both detectives knew that it would be better if Knuckles volunteered the information.

"But he's just a bookkeeper. He wouldn't have the balls to shoot Matty," Knuckles continued, as if he was thinking out loud.

"Well, let us be the judge of that, eh?" Stuart said, encouraging him. "Where do we find him?"

"Matty would phone him, and then he'd phone me and arrange to meet somewhere. I don't know where he lives or what he's done with the money, though."

"Alright, then, Knuckles. We'll leave it at that for now. Have a think, and if you want to speak to me, get them to call me," he said, nodding his head outside the cell towards the turnkeys who looked after the prisoners. "I'll mention to the guys that are dealing with your case that we've spoken to you, but we'll have to see if your information pans out."

"Okay, then, Mr Stuart. Thanks for trying to help."

"No worries, mate. You're helping yourself," Stuart said as they left the cell, clanging it shut behind them.

Stuart and Wilkinson looked at each other with beaming smiles on their faces and each knew what the other was thinking. Knuckles phone would hopefully have Whyte's mobile phone number on it, logged as a call received. With a little luck it would be the same number that was on Buchan's phone.

They both walked through to the cells complex office where they asked for Knuckles property record. After a few moments, the screen flashed up with details of a mobile phone that had been taken from him and retained within his property bag. Breaking the seal on it they rummaged through the items -- belt, tie, wallet, money, counted out and sealed in an envelope, jewellery – until they found his phone.

"You can't interrogate his phone," the turnkey cautioned them.

"We're only wanting his phone number so we can do the forms later, mate. Don't worry."

Chapter Nineteen

While Stuart and Wilkinson had been visiting Knuckles, Beattie and Reynold had also been hard at work. After having no luck in tracing Bill Whyte on any of the in-house computer systems, they had run his details through an internet search engine and had been surprised at how many times Bill Whyte appeared on Facebook, Twitter, LinkedIn, or any of the various news outlets that reported online. They had spent a fruitless day searching through the social media outlets trying to link up the phone number they had obtained for Whyte with the one displayed on the various websites that applied to the United Kingdom or to Scotland.

Collins meanwhile had also busied himself by contacting Greater Manchester Police who, he knew as a result of his time working at Edinburgh Airport as part of the response to the ongoing terrorism threats, held details of passenger manifests for most flights that left the United Kingdom. If someone had booked a flight online, the chances were that their details would be present with them.

Of course, travel agent bookings would not be so easily obtained, but many times in the past Collins and his then partner at the airport had been given the names and flight numbers of persons who were due to fly out on holiday, and who were the subject of outstanding warrants. An extract conviction warrant listed the amount of the fine that was to be paid, together with details of how long a period the person would have to spend in jail, should he or she choose to keep their money.

A Means Enquiry warrant also listed the amount of money that was due but, for various reasons, the offender had been given time to pay their fine but had failed to keep up with the payments. In either case, the person would not be flying unless they paid the whole amount there and then, and it was a wonderful lever to have at a cop's disposal, especially when everyone knew that they would be carrying their spending money.

Having contacted GMP, Collins easily found that Neilson had travelled three times in the past year, each time to Tenerife. He obtained as much detail as he could, including his passport number, the flight numbers and carrier of each flight he had made, and the days on which he had travelled. He was surprised to learn that Neilson had flown out two days before, again to Tenerife, on the day Copeland had been shot.

It was mid-morning when Stuart and Wilkinson called in to see them in their own offices, now close to where Superintendent McInnes had his office.

"How's it going, lads? Hard at work, I see," he said as he walked into the office.

"Morning, Willie," Reynolds said as he looked up from his monitor. "Aye, it's been a busy couple of days," he sighed, before updating the two of them as to how far they had progressed in tracing Whyte -- or not, as was actually the case.

"Ah, well, then. I think I can help you there," Stuart said, almost beaming. "Wilks and I have just been up at the cells speaking to Knuckles McNally, one of Buchan's enforcers. We picked up on the fact that he got lifted during the night and we had a wee chat with him. Your man Whyte is a bookkeeper or maybe an accountant."

"Ah! That makes a lot of sense. We found a few newspaper articles online about an accountant that got himself debarred, struck off, defrocked, or whatever the right term is. That was a couple of years back, though. We'll still need to identify the right Bill Whyte," he replied.

"I've got his phone number. Would that help?" Stuart asked.

"Is it the same as this one?" Reynolds replied, handing him a slip of paper with a telephone number on it, the one that he had previously called.

"It is, indeed."

"I'll get a data protection phone record form typed up and sent through to Mr McInnes ASAP, then. We have his number but we don't know who he is, what he looks like, where he lives, or where he works, though."

"Have you tried searching through the professional bodies that all these types of folks seem to join?" Wilks suggested.

"Well, not since you told me, no," Reynold said, laughing "We're going through the phone lists right now, so we'll put that on the to-do list."

"It looks like Neilson flew in and out of Tenerife about three times this year. He took a flight there in the last couple of days. According to GMP, there's a return flight in about a week," Collins chipped in.

"Really?" Stuart said, sounding surprised. "He booked it a while ago, did he?"

"No. Just in the last couple of days. Flew out of Edinburgh on the afternoon of the day Copeland got shot."

Stuart walked over to the door, closing it behind him as they walked in. He checked that it was closed properly.

"You know the HB at the house in Hawick -- the one where the rifle was stolen? Well, it is Neilson's print on the 'pick out' from the bit of glass that was found. We had it ID'd a couple of days ago, but we're still waiting on the paperwork to come back to us."

"I knew it. The bastard!" Collins exploded.

"That only goes to show he was there and maybe mixed up in a theft or an HB, Shug. Doesn't mean he used the rifle," Stuart reminded him.

"What about the car?" he asked. "Do you know where it went?" Collins asked.

"Nothing on the CCTV other than it turning off towards the bypass from the Wisp. But that's another reason we came down to see you. We're planning on going to the address to speak to the tenants. I've got a warrant typed up and signed off by the sheriff. We need to have a look in the garage."

"You want us to come with you?" Collins asked.

"Aye, I do. Have you got your authorisation to carry weapons through yet?"

"Yes, the operational order is in the file here," he replied, as he waved the file in Stuart's direction.

"Good. Then get yourselves squared away. We'll do an armed enquiry at the door and take it from there. If they don't have keys to the garage, we can break the lock off and have a shufftie."

"Can you give us fifteen or twenty minutes to get ready?"

"No problem. I'm going to go see McInnes, anyway," Stuart replied.

As Collins and Beattie left the office en route to the armoury to draw their Glock pistols, Stuart walked along the corridor to his boss's office.

"What's the story with Nielson, boss?" he asked him after he had closed the door behind him.

"I wish I knew. He's not on annual leave; he's not off sick, either."

"He's in Tenerife. The lads just told me a few minutes ago."

"Tenerife!" he roared, and then he composed himself. "Tenerife?"

Stuart then related what he had found out, what he had been told by his team, and what they intended to do.

"I agree. An armed enquiry, just to be on the safe side. Low-key, though, Willie. It's getting to be pretty close to home, and you remember what I said about it affecting the police."

Stuart nodded his agreement. "I'll let you know how we get on."

"How much of it can you prove right now, Willie?" McInnes asked.

"His prints are at the HB in Hawick. He could probably explain that. His name is in Docherty's notebook. He would have some explaining to do with that one. So there is nothing watertight just yet. I'm working on it, though. Hopefully, the house in Musselburgh will give us something."

All five of the Iago squad members rendezvoused at the traffic building, where they piled into an old unmarked car. Reynolds had called into his previous offices and collected a hit bag in case they stumbled over what they were looking for. The drive to Musselburgh did not take long, with the rush hour traffic having dissipated.

The address at Riverside Gardens in Musselburgh had been a semi-detached house on a single floor but had had an attic conversion built some years previously. There was no garage attached to it that they could see. Parking a short distance away, they walked to the front garden, surrounded by railings, with lawns on either side of the central path leading to the front door. It looked like a nice house.

With Collins and Beattie on either side of Stuart, they knocked on the front door. Police always preferred to knock. After a few moments, a flustered housewife came to the door, holding a baby in her arms.

"Mrs Cassiday?" Stuart asked.

"Yes, can I help you?" she replied.

Stuart introduced himself and his colleagues and then explained in bland terms the nature of their enquiry.

"You'd better come in," she said, turning to walk back into the house. "Excuse the mess, but the kids are off school with a stomach bug."

All three officers entered, allowing Stuart to lead the way. Collins and Beattie surveyed the house as they walked: A long hallway; bathroom at the far end with bedrooms off to the right, one front and one at the back; living room off to the left. On entering the lounge, they noted the extended kitchen at the rear of the house and a stairway, built immediately above the door, leading to an attic conversion and a third bedroom.

"Take a seat, please," she said. Helen Cassiday was young, perhaps thirty years old, petite with strawberry blond hair. "Would you like a cuppa?"

"Thank you, no," Stuart said. "You're obviously up to your eyes in it right now and we won't keep you long. I know it's hard when the kids are ill," he said, remembering his own experiences when his children were young.

"We understand the house is rented out to you by a Richard Neilson?"

"Yes, that's right."

"Is it just the house or are there any other outbuildings?"

"Just the house. There is a garage, but the landlord keeps that for himself."

"Do you deal with him directly or is it through a letting agency?"

"Through a letting agency, I think. If there's a problem, I phone them and they get a plumber or whatever to come and sort it."

"We're interested in an old Ford Fiesta car, green in colour. Have you ever seen it parked here?"

"I can't say I have, no. The parking in the street is pretty bad. Several of the houses have built driveways off the street, as there's so many that get parked here at night."

"That's fine, then, Mrs Cassiday. We're interested in the garage and not the house. Where is the garage?"

"It's down the side of next door," she pointed to the left at the front of the house. "Just a minute's walk."

"Thank you for your help," they said, as they rose and left the house to walk to where she had indicated.

The track lead to a series of buildings, lock-ups more than garages, and it was obvious to the officers that the local council did not cover the upkeep of the area, as the "road" was potholed and filled in with hard core. Reynold followed them with the car as they walked past the lock-ups, looking for an identifying number that would point them in the right direction.

Several of the lock-ups had been well-used, judging by the worn, hard-packed earth at the entrance door. Others had grass and weeds growing underfoot. Stuart reached into his jacket pocket and pulled out a copy of the Sasines Register he had obtained and looked at it again. The separate purchase of the garage had been made several years back with only a reference to "Garage 6," indicating which it might be.

Was it number 6 from the left or number 6 from the right, though? He thought to himself, looking up and down the row of lock-ups. *Eleven lock-ups in all. So 6 from the left is the same as 6 from the right.*

"This one" he said to Collins, as he waved Reynolds forwards and indicated where he should park. Going to the boot of the car, he brought out the hit bag and withdrew a large pair of heavy bolt cutters, snipping though the small padlock easily. He then stepped back. Collins and Beattie opened the door, making sure to remain behind it as they did so. There was the green Fiesta, and the registration number was spot on.

"Bingo," Collins said.

"Bingo, right enough," Stuart agreed. "Johnny, get the ID branch down here. We need this car to be forensically recovered and the area around it, too."

"I'll get that organised, boss," he replied. "Is the car open, though? We'll need to get into it if it isn't."

Stuart and Collins opened both garage doors wide and could see that it was in a state of disrepair, with thick dust on the floor, cobwebs hanging from the roof, and damp patches on the walls. Looking at the floor, they could clearly see the outline of footprints in the dust at the driver's door and towards the rear of the car that had been reversed in.

Stuart knew immediately that he shouldn't disturb anything and that he ought not to walk down that side of the vehicle. Walking carefully up the passenger side of the vehicle where the dust lay undisturbed, he tried the front and rear passenger doors. They were locked.

He then had an idea. Taking a piece of string, he tied a knot in one end and then carefully shuffled down the driver's side of the car to where the boot impression lay. Without disturbing the outline, he measured the footprint by holding the knot in the string at one end and tying another knot at the other. It was an old trick he had learned many years before, when access to photographing crime scenes had been limited.

"I think it's all locked up, assuming that, even for an old car, it's got central locking," he said over his shoulder to his colleagues, who stood back outside the door.

"What about getting a traffic car down here? They used to carry "Slim Jims" for getting into cars. I'm not sure if they do that anymore, but they might have tape if the internal release on the door is the right kind," Collins suggested.

A Slim Jim was a long piece of thin, bendable metal, similar to a foot ruler, with a notch cut into one end. In experienced hands, the Slim Jim could be inserted down the inside of the rubber seal of the window, just above the lock, and then dragged back to the lock and across the locking mechanism within the door frame, where the notch would hopefully connect with and release the lock.

The tape that Collins referred to was ordinary packing-case tape, the kind that secured boxes of A4 paper. Again, in experienced hands, the tape could be used to open car locks, whereby the door was levered back at the top slightly, and the tape, doubled over and with a small kink inserted at the end, could be slid down from the top of the door to the bottom and then the doubled-over end pushed and pulled so that there was a loop formed on the inside of the car. This loop was then cajoled into place over the top of the internal lock release, tightened and the pulled sharply.

It frequently worked, but the "snib" on the inside had to be wider at the top than at the bottom so that some purchase could be gained. In newer cars, this couldn't be done anymore as the manufacturers had learned their lessons.

"Wrong kind of locks. Hopefully, they'll have a Slim Jim. I don't want our fingerprints all over the car -- not just yet, anyway," he replied.

Stuart came back out and looked about the garages area. There were several houses with rough-and-ready driveways built at the rear, some of which overlooked the area. These people would have to be spoken to, and he asked Beattie to note the numbers of the houses that might be of value when their occupiers were interviewed by the murder squad detectives later, to see if they had seen the vehicle being used and by whom.

It didn't take long for the traffic vehicle to arrive, but the crew of two, an old-school traffic officer and his younger partner, didn't have the required gadgets.

"Okay, then," Stuart said to his assembled team. "Can a couple of you wait here for the ID Branch to attend? Get them to photograph everything they can. Have them fingerprint the car here before anyone else has touched it, then get it picked up and brought to HQ where they can have a really good go at it, and see what we can get back."

"You want it lifted onto the back of a flat-bed truck?" Collins asked.

"Aye, that'll do nicely. I'll head back to the squad with Wilks. Can you guys stay here with the car? Get Jamie to send me details of the addresses overlooking this area," he said, waving his hand in a 180-degrees arc.

"No problem, Boss. We'll jump in with the truck driver and get a lift back to HQ. We can let you know how it pans out."

"Sounds like a plan, lads." Stuart said, before jumping into his car and driving off.

Chapter Twenty

Howard William Whyte had been a chartered accountant with a well-to-do family firm in Edinburgh for a few years when he had taken on a client whom he had reservations about. But, as he had been new to the company and was keen to impress them with his business acumen and abilities, he had neglected to pay the strictest attention to the money laundering legislation that should have been a warning signal to him.

Each new client was required to be subjected to an initial and, thereafter on-going, risk assessment with regard to their perhaps onerous or pressurised requirements, or their uncooperative or secretive behaviour. The firm's customer due-diligence regulations covered three components: They should know who the clients were and be able to confirm their identities by checking reliable and independent documentation; they should ascertain and verify who was benefitting from the business and who the ultimate owners of the business were; and they should know what the purpose of the business relationship was and what the client expected the company to do.

Whyte had been right to suspect the intentions of Enoch McNally when he was approached by him with a request to look after the company books of "McNally Security."

He answered all the questions Whyte had asked at their initial meeting and had produced the required documents relating to his ownership of the company and his own identity. He had, however, been secretive regarding the number of his employees, their expected salaries, and the number of contracts they had in place to supply doormen at various nightclubs.

Whyte had become concerned regarding a number of cheques that had been made out to McNally's firm, often from the same club, for larger and larger amounts. His suspicions grew when McNally brought in large quantities of money for him to pay in through his firm's accounts. He hadn't done so, of course, but had chosen to put the cash into his own bank accounts, much to his later regret.

As time went on, McNally no longer called in to see him when requested to explain some of the facts and figures that he submitted. Whyte had tried to raise the matter with his superiors in the firm and had lied when asked if he had completed his "KYC" – Know Your Client. He knew that he had not completed a request for disclosure of McNally's convictions be handed in for him to examine.

If he had, he wouldn't have placed himself or the firm in the situation that they now found themselves in -- laundering the proceeds of crime through a supposedly legitimate company. As McNally Security's first year of trading came to an end, it was apparent that their turnover was huge, in spite of it being a small company with a small number of staff, something that was never explained by McNally when asked.

Whyte's deception was uncovered following an internal audit of the risk assessments made during the year, and he had been the subject disciplinary review. In view of his failure to check all the details of the company, no checks with credit institutions having been undertaken and no senior management approval having been sought, Whyte was judged to have brought reputational damage to the company, and he was fired.

The police were informed about his involvement with McNally's company, and he was detained and interviewed at length. He had been released without charge, however, having apparently satisfied the officers that he was unaware of the real nature of McNally's business and who was behind it. He had been stupid, he now knew, and should have asked more questions before refusing to have any dealings with him.

He supplied the police with as much information as he could, as did his previous employers, but he suspected that McNally would come looking for him sooner rather than later, in an effort to learn what he had divulged. As a married man with a mortgage and young family, with no means of support, he had again been approached by McNally, this time with Matty Buchan at his side. Invited to carry on his work as before, he knew that he was in over his head but also knew that he could do very little about it. What else could he do but say, "Yes."

Over the next few years, he was drawn further and further into the web of intrigue that he was reluctantly helping to weave. Buchan was a very smart man and learned quickly the many different ways which he could have his money squirrelled away. He just needed someone at arm's length from him who would be able to keep track of it all and, besides, Whyte was well-paid for what he was doing.

Buchan instructed several of his many contacts to open up bank accounts in their own names but made sure that all the account details, the bank cards used to withdraw and deposit money, as well as details required to access the accounts online, were passed to him. When the dealers he used to distribute his drugs had sold their stock, they would be told to deposit the money in one or two of these accounts.

Whyte was instructed thereafter to quickly transfer some or all of the money into a secondary account, or even a tertiary account, from where it could be transferred abroad to offshore accounts, or cash could be taken and deposited in Buchan's well-hidden accounts in false names.

Whyte also made sure that Buchan did not own anything on paper, leasing large and powerful cars – a status symbol -- through one of the accounts which he knew the police might want to know about and how he could afford to have such vehicles. But he also knew that police couldn't take it from him, as it was still owned by the company leasing the vehicle. They didn't have and would not get his account details.

Buchan diversified into cash-intensive businesses, taking over laundrettes (where the term "money laundering" was derived), car washes, and taxi firms. Each of these enterprises could never be audited properly by the taxman as there was always the possibility of busy times and quiet times. It was easy for cash from the drug trade to be added to the day's takings and paid into the respective business accounts, provided that it was done on a regular basis, in a controlled manner.

In this respect, Whyte excelled. As long as the tax returns for each company were reasonable and not excessive, the taxman would not come back to them, wanting a closer inspection of their trading activities. A partnership or a sole trader didn't require a qualified accountant, registered with a governing body, to look after their books. In fact, it could be done by anyone online with access to the account with HMRC.

But Whyte was very conscious that he knew everything that Buchan knew and, what was more, he had it written down in ledgers. He realised that he would have to make preparations for his retirement, or at least a way out of what he was doing, and should take steps to protect himself, as he saw it, from Buchan and his team of heavies.

His illegal activities weighed heavily on his mind and, apart from two brushes with the law -- once when he was at school and the one when he got fired -- he had never been in trouble with the police.

To this end, he began to make copies of his ledgers and used his accountancy skills to hide money in plain sight, something that he knew only a skilled practitioner would be able to unravel. By undervaluing the depreciation of the individual company's assets and overvaluing the repairs to machinery or the wastage accrued by the materials that they used, he pocketed the difference, along with money skimmed off the top of the cash that Buchan dropped off with him. Buchan was smart, certainly, but he couldn't remember everything.

A short time afterwards, he accidently hit upon a failsafe opportunity. As a very popular destination town with three universities, Edinburgh was awash with foreign students. On the completion of their studies, many students returned home and simply left their accounts open. The accounts that Buchan's team of dealers had opened were always vulnerable to being discovered when the Police came calling with their drugs warrants, but a foreign student was unlikely to come back and reuse his or her old account, especially when they had sold it before going home.

Asking McNally and his staff to make enquiries of the regular students frequenting the nightclubs when they were going home, they began to obtain details that they needed and were able to secure several account details, bank cards, and PIN numbers in return for a small outlay. Keeping the details of these accounts, he made Buchan aware of some of them but kept a few back for personal use, particularly the ones with internet access.

Making sure to keep the money moving through various accounts, he ensured that the trail was a very difficult one to follow. Although Buchan and his close group were always roughly aware of what they were earning, Whyte ensured that he kept them in an affluent lifestyle, whilst at the same time skimming money and hiding it in various in accessible places.

It had been a chance meeting with an old school friend that caused him to realise just how far Buchan's network stretched. Flying out to Tenerife on a family holiday, he had bumped into Rich Neilson who was also going on holiday to the same resort. They met up when they were there and talked over old times, promised to keep in touch with each other, and, as their renewed acquaintance grew, they each opened up about their lives since they had left school.

Neilson had heard about Whyte's fall from grace within the accountancy world, as it had appeared in the papers at the time. Sympathising, Neilson had mentioned the events at school where Buchan had been the fall guy for their collective smoking of cannabis on the school grounds and where Whyte had also been one of the witnesses against him.

"It's a small world, isn't it?" he had suggested. "Buchan's still got a hold on me, even now. A scary bloke that just doesn't take 'no' for an answer."

"You, too?" Whyte had replied, with each of them wary of revealing just what it was that they had done or were being forced to do.

"We'll keep in touch when we get back to the UK," Neilson had suggested as they swapped phone numbers.

"Certainly," Whyte had agreed. "I'm looking for a change in career, but I'm not sure which direction to go or how I should do it. Perhaps with your police connections, you could help me, and I might be able to help you, too."

Chapter Twenty-One

It hadn't taken long for the Identification Branch team to attend at the lock-up. They photographed the boot impressions in the dust on the floor, which could prove to be important if the boots were recovered and their ownership established later. They covered the Ford Fiesta vehicle in aluminium powder, looking for any fingerprints, well-knowing that what was inside the car was of more importance.

After all, anyone could have touched the car. It had been dragged out of the lock-up by a winch, up onto a flatbed lorry, where it was taken to Police HQ and placed in a securely locked area within the police car park, but under cover in order that the vehicle would not be tampered with. Beattie and Collins travelled with the car and, on arrival, had located a "Slim Jim" from their traffic colleagues. Their use frowned upon these days by senior officers, but nevertheless, they came in handy on occasion. An old Sergeant had one in the bottom drawer of his desk.

The following day, Beattie and Collins were both standing by the car when the ID Branch lads turned up in their white paper suits. Entry had already been gained to the car but they hadn't gone inside. They had had a look in the boot compartment to see if there was perhaps a rifle there. Neither had been surprised to see that it was empty. The ID branch fingerprinted the inside of the vehicle, with particular attention to the smooth surfaces that would retain any impressions, such as the rear view mirror and the insides of the windows.

As would be expected, there were several sets of impressions recovered that would be examined and possibly identified in due course. They also took samples of the dried mud or dust that was on the mats on the floor and pedals of the car in order to make comparisons at a later date, should they be given samples to compare them against. That was part and parcel of the job, they knew. Take what you could find, however meaningless it might seem at the time. There was always the chance that something might turn up, sometimes a long time after the event.

Whilst this was being done, Stuart was on the phone to McInnes, updating him on the latest developments in the Buchan case and enquiring of him as to how the Copeland case was progressing.

"Has it given you a breakthrough?" McInnes asked about the recovered car.

"Not yet, if at all. The car was clean and tidy on the inside; there was nothing in any of the glove compartments that would give us a clue as to who was driving or using it. There's load of prints on the outside of the car and probably a few internally, too. They'll have to be examined and identified. There wasn't any weapon in the boot of the car either. It's just going to be a little while until we get the results. How's the Copeland case going? Is there a link yet?"

"It's not looking like it, Willie," McInnes replied. "As you know, they recovered a shell casing with a partial print on it. They've done a search against it but come up with nothing. I even asked them to check against police records, just in case. I told them to do that as it's not the first time something has been found with police prints all over it."

"You were hoping that they would be Neilson's?"

"It would've made our lives so much simpler Willie. But they're not his. You just keep on with what you're doing and keep me updated".

"You think that it's time that we did Neilson's house? See what we can come up with," Stuart asked.

"I can't see you getting a warrant for that, Willie. We have a print at an HB two years ago and it was identified, probably illegally. We can't search the records of someone who doesn't have pre-cons and use it in court for identification purposes, as you are aware. As far as I know, nobody has identified him driving the Fiesta either, and the images of the man in black on the night of Buchan's murder are not great."

"I agree, but it's good to get independent thoughts on it," Stuart responded. "I've got a lot on my plate right now."

"You and me both, Willie. You and me both. I'll speak to you later."

Stuart leaned back in his chair again and tried to calm his mind and think clearly.

If we get Interpol involved, Neilson will know we're after him. But we need to find him, nevertheless. We need to find Bill Whyte and try make a connection to Neilson, Buchan, and the rest of them, he thought to himself.

Sitting upright once more, he picked up the phone and called the offices of Operation Iago.

"3281" was the reply, as Jamie Beattie answered.

Good lad, Stuart thought to himself. He had given nothing away. It could have been a wrong number, after all.

"Jamie? It's Willie."

"Hi there, Boss. What can I do for you?"

"Just looking for an update on how you're getting on at your end."

"Pretty good, actually. We were going to give you a bell at close of play tonight, but we might as well tell you now." Beattie waited for a response but realised that he should just carry on.

"Bill Whyte is not William Whyte. He's Howard William Whyte. We found him while checking the newspapers and online stuff from a few years back."

"And?" Stuart asked, getting impatient.

"Seems he was an accountant with a firm. He got himself mixed up with a dodgy client and got himself fired. He was brought in by the Fraud Squad guys and interviewed but was released without charge. The good news is that he was put into the custody system as Howard William Whyte, and we found his record. That's why we couldn't find him under just William. The system won't search for partial names unless you specifically ask it to."

"Go on," Stuart encouraged him.

"We have an address for him but we don't know if it's current. It was from four or five years back. But we can do a voter roll check and look for him on all the social media stuff that folks sign up to these days. We'll find him that way. We also accessed the intelligence reports that the Fraud Squad guys put in, and they make some interesting reading, too. Seems that Whyte spilled his guts about everything he knew. Pretty much bared his soul by all accounts."

"He talked about the approach by Enoch McNally and doing the security company books, the secretive nature of him, the cash that was coming in with the cheques from the clubs getting larger and larger for such a small company. Seems he tried to get out by speaking with his bosses, but he hadn't done all the checks that he should have done."

"And McNally works for Buchan. We knew that, but he didn't," Stuart suggested. "What about Neilson?"

"We have his passport number. We got a fax through from GMP with his flight details and passport number. We should be able to trace his movements leaving the country with our Border Force chums. But we won't know what he gets up to when he leaves the country, though."

"Agreed" Stuart said in monotone, thinking what his next move would be.

"Alrighty. We've been at this pretty hard over the last couple of days. You lot take a couple of days off and get some rest. I'll speak with McInnes again, but I think it's about time we had a chat with Mr Whyte. If he burst the last time he was lifted, he might do so again. Tell the rest of the boys, 'well done' from me."

Chapter Twenty-Two

Howard Whyte was indeed easily found. The information relating to his comfortable address on Colinton Road in Edinburgh had been found on the voters roll and was waiting on Beattie, Collins, and Reynolds when they returned to the office after their time off. Unlike his business associates who were not registered voters and therefore invisible for liability for various local taxes, Whyte and his wife paid their dues and did their civic duty.

After making a quick phone call to Willie Stuart informing him of the latest development and asking him how he wished for them to proceed, John Reynolds was soon busy at work making an application for a warrant to search Whyte's address. Gone were the days when a warrant could just be typed up and a justice of the peace approached. Warrants were required to be evidenced-based, sworn out before a sheriff, and it took a considerable amount of time and effort for them to gather the required intelligence material that had been gleaned from McNally, the phone records, and the intelligence relating to Whyte's previous detention.

When they were ready, Reynolds contacted the Procurator Fiscal and obtained permission to approach a sheriff, whilst Beattie and Collins organised a team of search officers who could assist them if Whyte was not forthcoming with the documentation that they hoped he would have. There was always the chance that he would not keep it at home with him. He might also have an office somewhere that they did not know about.

It was after eleven in the morning when they were ready to move to the address. A Monday morning was always a busy time at Court with all the people that had been locked up over the weekend appearing at their first Diet in order to establish who would admit their guilt and who wouldn't. Those who didn't admit their crimes would be required to appear at a later date, but then again, most of those who did also had to come back, too.

Stuart was contacted again and updated, but he declined the use of a search team, wanting instead to keep it amongst themselves due to the nature of the enquiry and McInnes' instruction. He and Jim Wilkinson would meet them at the address in a separate vehicle and they would interview Whyte if they managed to get a hold of him. Beattie and Collins drew their firearms as per their standing orders and joined Reynold in the car park a short time later.

Colinton Road, a long arterial route from the south into central Edinburgh, was an affluent area with many stone-built bungalows and school playing fields dotted around. Unfortunately, large portions of some of the playing fields had been sold off for housing development and, as was the case many times over the years, the local council had built large housing estates on the open land that had once made the area so attractive. They had also sold off the land to private house builders and now, as a result, the traffic increased with the developments and buses ran 24-7.

Pulling up short of the address Stuart and Wilks sat waiting on the others to arrive.

"We'll need Whyte to decode the books for us," Wilks suggested. "It would take our guys ages to do it, and I'm not talking about Shug, Jamie, or John. Even our experts would take some time."

"I agree, but he burst the last time he spoke to the police. He'll maybe do it again if we play our cards right," Stuart said, as the car with the others pulled up behind them. All five met up on the pavement and discussed what they were going to do.

Stuart began, "As an apparently fine, upstanding member of the community, we have no intelligence about the lay out of the house. Whyte has never been arrested, after all. The only thing at the back of my mind is that one of Buchan's crew might be in attendance and that would cause problems. It ain't gonna be Knuckles. He got remanded and Matty's dead. I don't think that Docherty knows about Whyte either, so we should be okay, unless we're really unlucky and someone that we don't know about has turned up. Just to be on the safe side, though, Jamie, you go to the back with John, if you can get there. Shug, you come with Wilks and me to the front door."

With that, Jamie and John walked off to see if they could get to the rear of the house. As they passed the front garden gate to the semi-detached house, they could see that there was a path around the side of it. Several of the houses had had full fences put in place to try to prevent locals from gaining access to the rear of the properties, thereby acting as a crime-prevention measure. No one would break in through the front of a house on such a busy road, after all. Looking back to Stuart, Jamie gave a thumbs-up sign to him as he entered through the gate. Stuart and his team walked to the address.

Knocking on the front door, they waited for a few moments and could hear various doors opening and footsteps coming from inside. Collins stood slightly back with his hand on the Glock pistol, still within its holster under his jacket.

A small-statured man, perhaps in his early thirties, with a shock of blond hair answered the door.

"Can I help you?" he asked in a quiet voice.

"Howard Whyte?" Stuart asked, glancing at Collins, who nodded back at him, signifying that that was the face he had seen on the social media outlets.

"I'm DI Stuart -- Detective Inspector Stuart," he said, showing him his warrant card identification. "Could we come in, please? We have something that we have to discuss with you."

"Ah, I've been expecting you to come. Yes, come in."

As they followed Whyte, they were all attentive to the layout of the house.

"Are you alone at home today, Mr Whyte?" Stuart asked.

"Right now, yes. The kids are at school and my wife is out at her part time job. I work from home."

Wilks and Stuart looked at each other, both thinking the same thing. *Great. He's volunteering information already. And we haven't even started yet.*

"I should tell you that we have a couple of police out the back of your property. Can I get them to come to the front?"

"Yes, please do. The kitchen is right there," Whyte said, indicating the door with a pointed finger.

Collins went through and waved at his colleagues to come to the front and allow themselves entry.

"Five of you? This must be serious," Whyte offered, trying to make a thin joke of the situation in which he found himself.

"Well, to be frank, Mr Whyte, if you were expecting us, I guess you know why we're here."

"Matthew Buchan, by any chance?"

"Indeed. I should also tell you that we have a warrant to search your house and that we will want to speak to you at the station."

"Is it the books that you're after? The ones that I keep for Buchan's businesses?" Whyte asked.

"Correct. Would you like to give us them now?"

"Yes, they're through there," he said, pointing in the direction of a small study off the hallway. "I knew that it was only a matter of time until you guys came calling, after what happened to Buchan. I'm only glad it was you and not some of the men that Buchan employs. I've been living in terror the last couple of weeks, wondering what was going to happen to me and my family."

"I know, I know," Stuart said, trying his best to sound sympathetic to Whyte's predicament. *But if you fly with the crows, you'll get shot down with the crows, too,* he thought to himself.

Whyte just hung his head down low, bringing his hands up to either side and sighed deeply.

"We need the account books, and we need you to explain the contents to us. Can you do that?" Stuart asked.

"Yes, yes, of course. I'll get them," he said, as he rose and walked out of the lounge. Collins followed him and saw that he lifted up several box folders, two or three large ledgers, and a ring binder from the desk in the office. Collins noted that there was a computer terminal installed.

"This is what you want. It's all here," he said, offering it to Stuart. Reynolds and Wilks took them and opened them up to have quick looks through them. Cash deposits, names, dates, and company names were all listed in the ledgers. In the ring binder were pages of plastic sleeves with bank cards, together with account names, sorting codes, and PIN numbers, with access details for internet banking. The box folders were full of lists of names that had been typed up with details of money either paid or due to them, with weights and measures of the various drugs that had been purchased or sold.

"Thank you," Stuart said. "Do you have any large amounts of cash here?"

"No. No, I don't. I didn't think that it would be wise to keep any money here, especially after Buchan got shot, and I didn't know who would be coming here."

"Okay, then. That's fine. You're cooperating with us, which is great. Thanks for that, but we'll have to have a look around just to make sure. We'll take your computer, and we'll need details of your own bank accounts. Just to dot the 'Is' and cross the 'Ts,' you understand."

Stuart wasn't stupid enough to think that a crooked accountant would actually keep stolen, appropriated, or illegally earned money in his own bank account, but it might prove useful later if he couldn't explain how he managed to sustain his family without a full-time occupation.

"Do you have a job, or do you just work for Buchan?"

"Just Buchan. Have you ever met him? He's one of these people, these scary people, that you just can't say 'no' to."

"I know him, or should I say, knew him. I knew him well. And I agree with you -- a scary bloke. Was it him that you dealt with? Was there anyone else?"

"Mainly him and McNally. I don't think that many people around him knew what I was doing.

"These are very thorough," Wilks said to Whyte, "at least to my eye."

"I try to be. Years of training, I suppose. That, and the fact that I wanted to keep a record in case something like this happened. It was the only thing that I could think of to do in order to protect myself and my family."

As they talked together in the lounge, the other officers quickly searched the house in a cursory manner, looking in cupboards, wardrobes, and under beds purely to satisfy themselves, but all five of them felt sure that Whyte was telling the truth and was looking for a way out as painlessly as possible. After about fifteen or twenty minutes they were satisfied.

"What time does your wife get back from work?"

"She picks the kids up from school first, about three or three-thirty."

"That's fine, then. I didn't want them to be locked out when we leave here," Stuart wanted to help him as much as he could, knowing that Whyte would appreciate the small kindness.

"Right, then," he said to Whyte. "We're going to detain you under the Criminal Procedure (Scotland) Act 1995, Section 14, regarding money laundering offences. You will be asked questions regarding this. You don't have to answer these questions, but if you do, your replies with be recorded, noted, and may be used as evidence. Do you understand?"

"Yes, I do."

"You can have an interview with a lawyer before any interview with us, have the lawyer present with you when you are interviewed, or you can choose not to have one. But that'll be explained at the station."

"I don't think I need one. I want to get this off my chest," he admitted.

"Well, we'll ask you again, anyway. You can get in touch with your wife later, too, and tell her what's happened."

The officers gathered up the evidence that they had been given, with Collins carrying the computer base unit, as they walked to the cars and drove off to the cells complex.

On arrival, Whyte was processed, declining to have a solicitor informed of his detention but asking that his wife be informed. He was then placed in a holding cell whilst the Iago Squad members began pouring over the books and ledgers, making notes about the names of the accounts and the amounts that each held.

Hopefully, Whyte's computer would reveal the extent to which he had been transferring money backwards and forwards via the internet. There was a lot of money involved, certainly hundreds of thousands of pounds, if not millions. It would take a forensic accountant some time to unravel the entries in the ledgers and follow the trail left behind.

When Stuart and Wilks had satisfied themselves that they had a reasonable idea of what he had been up to, they went back to the cells and spoke with Whyte. Having set up the interview room with both audio and DVD playback, they spoke with him for several hours, only stopping for breaks for cups of coffee or something to eat, as well as bathroom breaks.

And Whyte was as good as his word, if that was worth anything at this present moment in his life. He spoke about all the transactions he could remember, and the ones he could not, he jogged his memory by reference to the ledgers. He explained how they had come by the various accounts that they had used and where he knew the money was coming from.

He made reference to accounts in the British Virgin Islands that he had set up for Buchan and his wife, but that Buchan kept the details of his internet access to them a closely guarded secret, and something that he had most likely taken to his grave. Of course, Whyte knew about them; he had set them up, after all. He even included the accounts that he was using himself as a means of taking money from Buchan in case he had to leave Edinburgh quickly.

Where he would go and how he would do it, he had no idea, he admitted to them.

At the conclusion of the interview, Stuart and Wilks thanked him for his honesty in the matter.

"Until this point, Howard" Stuart told him, "you have been detained. I am now going to formally arrest you. You do not have to say anything but anything you do say will be noted and may be used in evidence."

He again declined the services of a solicitor but asked that his wife be informed as it was now after seven pm, and she would be worried about him.

He was then charged with offences under the Proceeds of Crime Act 2002, Section 327, regarding his concealing, disguising, converting, or transferring of criminal property. Whyte made no reply, just hanging his head and shaking it from side to side. The two officers brought him back through to the counter where his updated status was recorded on the force computer system and the charge added.

"We're not in a position to report him right now, Willie," Wilks whispered to his boss. "He'll only get released in the morning pending an appearance at a later date, anyway."

"You're right, Jimmy. We'll release him and take him home. We'll get his passport so he can't leave the country, and we'll get him to sign on at a station every couple of days or once a week or whatever."

After the system had been updated, Whyte was fingerprinted and had his DNA and photograph taken, and then Collins and Beattie gave him a lift home, obtaining his passport and that of his wife, too.

Chapter Twenty-Three

"He's been fucking what!" McInnes exploded, seething with anger when told that Whyte had been released and then later identified.

"Yeah, it seems that after Willie Stuart had interviewed Howard Whyte yesterday and then released him, his fingerprints, which had been input directly into the system were compared against all those outstanding unidentified ones. He was a direct hit for the prints on the shell casing for our enquiry," the SIO of the Copeland case said down the line to McInnes. "Oh, and the bullets that were found at our locus came from the same weapon that was used at Buchan's shooting. I just got the analysis report from the firearms experts."

"Christ Almighty." McInnes paused and thought quickly. "Right, then. Get a couple of officers round to his house as soon as you can. In fact, even better, get a couple of uniform cops round there now to at least keep tabs on the house. Get him, and get him interviewed again. Get on it," he replied before putting the phone down.

You'd better have a good reason for letting him go, Willie, he thought to himself as he dialled the Murder Squad number looking for him.

"DI Stuart."

"Willie, I've just had Davie Grant from the Copeland Squad on the phone. Did you know that your man Whyte's prints are on the shell casing found at his locus?"

"They're fucking what?" Stuart shouted down the phone.

"Yeah, that's what I just said to Davie. He's been identified from the prints that you took off him yesterday. What did you let him go for?"

"The bastard," Stuart cursed. "The little bastard. We released him for summons, Boss," picking up on McInnes' anger and trying to assuage it. He continued, "We weren't in a position to report him. The books and ledgers that we got off him will take a good while to put into some semblance of order for court purposes, and we'll have to get someone who will be able to speak to their contents in court and put in a statement to that effect. It'll probably need someone from outside the force to do that -- an expert in accountancy.

"Then, there was how he handed everything over to us, spoke freely for a few hours, and told us everything. We got his passport so he can't leave the country, as well. And that's before all the other stuff that we're doing right now to try find Buchan's killer. We kinda got side-tracked by this Neilson carry-on, but the Squad have still been soldiering on with their enquiries. Besides, if you wanted a link between both cases, I would suggest that you have one now."

"Well, that's confirmed now. There's a striation match on the bullets recovered from Copeland's locus with the one that was found at yours. They were both fired from the same gun," McInnes informed him.

Every rifled gun barrel that has the rotational grooves imparts spin to a bullet in order to improve accuracy during flight, leaving corresponding grooves and lands on the bullet that has been fired. As each barrel is unique, it can be ascertained with certainty which rifle had fired the shot. It had been a fairly simple process to compare each recovered round for similarities.

"Oh, Christ. It's a drugs war, then, in addition to everything else that's going on. Someone's trying to take over in Edinburgh," Stuart said.

"We'll just have to keep an open mind on that, Willie," McInnes responded, his anger subsiding at the well-rounded thought processes that he had been given in response to his question. "Let's find out who's done the shooting first and then take it from there. But listen, I think you're right about all the other stuff that you're doing. I'll get Davie Grant to take over your enquiry. You'll still be deputy SIO, but you need a bit of help to wade through all the paper."

"Yes, fine with me, Boss. And rest assured, once Whyte's been interviewed by the Copeland Team, I'll be in there right at the back of them with a few questions of my own."

When he had hung up the phone, Stuart leaned back in his chair. He considered himself to be an excellent judge of character. How could he have got it wrong? Had he got him wrong? No, he was sure that Whyte would be at home; wouldn't he?

The uniformed panda car that was dispatched to Whyte's address took up observations and sat waiting on the CID officers to arrive. Two vehicles soon parked up, and the cops watched as they went to the house. After a few moments, Whyte came to the door and he was soon detained a second time. The uniform officers were then asked to remain in situ whilst a warrant to search the house was carved and they were handed a set of keys to the property. A search team would be with them shortly, they were told, and permission to search the house without the occupier being present had been granted.

On arrival at the cells, Whyte was processed as before, but this time he asked that Willie Stuart be informed of his detention and that he wanted to speak with him before the officers who had detained him interviewed him regarding his involvement in the shootings. But it was McInnes who phoned Stuart first to let him know that Whyte had been detained and that, as both enquiries were now linked, he and DCI Davie Grant would interview Whyte.

Stuart made his way to the cells complex where he met up with Davie Grant, and they conferred for a considerable time as to the evidence that they had gathered from their respective enquiries. They were sitting in the interview room when Whyte was shown in. Stuart was keenly aware that McInnes had told him previously to keep the Neilson portion of his investigation under the strictest of wraps, and he had been thinking about how he was going to speak to Whyte without mentioning it. He decided that he wouldn't say anything but that if Whyte mentioned anything to do with Neilson, he would cross that bridge when he came to it.

"Howard, this is becoming a regular occurrence," Stuart said as he entered the room. "I thought you had told us everything yesterday."

"I didn't know that I had been set up, though. It wasn't me. Honestly, it wasn't me." He implored Stuart to believe him.

"Just take a seat, Howard. We'll get to that."

After going through the interview protocols, Stuart and Grant explained again that he had been detained in connection with the murder of Daniel Copeland. The officers asked him to account for his movements on the day before and on the day that Copeland was shot and only interjected to clarify particular points as he relayed his story.

It was difficult for them to follow as Whyte was speaking rapidly, and he had to be asked to slow down for the benefit of the recordings that were being made. A transcript would have to be typed up verbatim, in due course, and everything had to be as clear as possible for Court.

"So where were you on the morning that Dan Copeland was shot?" Grant asked him.

"I was at home. I work from home."

"Can anyone verify that?"

"My wife can."

"What about someone independent?"

"I had a boiler and central heating servicing appointment through the gas board that day. I think it was in the morning. They'll be able to tell you that I let the guy into the house. And I signed the forms once they had done their thing."

"How can you account for your fingerprints being on the shell casing that was found at the locus of the shooting, then?"

"The only thing I can say is that might have been when I picked some up when Rich Neilson spilled them when he came around to the house."

Stuart sat back in his chair and thought to himself, *You devious little bastard. There's the connection that I've been looking for. Why couldn't you have said that yesterday?*

"Rich Neilson?" Grant asked, not making the connection as his attention was focussed on his enquiry.

"Yes, a friend from my school days. We happened to bump into each other a while back when we went on holiday. We got talking about the old days. We were both at school with Matthew Buchan, you see."

"Go on," Stuart encouraged him, hoping that he wouldn't notice his jaw was clamped tight as he seethed with anger.

"It transpired that we were both in debt to Buchan," he continued. "Rich was getting blackmailed and I needed work to keep the family together. I couldn't get it through the normal channels after I got fired, and then he came looking for me to carry on doing his books and hiding his money. He's a very hard man to say 'no' to. You need to understand that."

"And that's the books that you talked to me about yesterday?"

"Yes."

"So," Stuart continued, "what about these bullets?"

"Rich came to the house when my wife was at work about two or three months back and said that he had a plan where we could both get away from Buchan. He told me that he was going to plant some bullets in Buchan's car and let the police know when he was driving it, using some of his police connections. They would take it from there. He opened up his briefcase to explain what he was going to do and some of the bullets spilled out. I picked them up for him and put them back into the box."

"Did he ask you to pick them up?"

"No I did it. I just thought that it was a clumsy accident."

"What makes you think that it wasn't now" Stuart asked "What makes this so memorable?"

"I'd never seen or handled bullets before, or since. He visited me often after that and we spoke about how we would be able to get away from Buchan's influence. But the conversation always came back to the money from Buchan's dealings, which account had the most money in it, and the accounts I had set up for him in the Virgin

Islands. He wanted to know how I had done it. I thought that that was a bit strange, to be honest, but I'd known him for years, and I wanted away from Buchan desperately.

"Neilson wanted to know about how much of Buchan's money was hidden. He said that he would use it to trap Buchan, and I showed him the folder with the account details and the cards in the sleeves a few times. But a short time after that, I noticed that some of the money had been taken out the accounts and paid into accounts in the name of Steven Randall, in several branches of several different banks in and around Edinburgh. I checked the files and the cards were still there, but the authorisation card reader device was missing. I thought I'd just mislaid it and ordered another. In the week that the new reader took to arrive, most of the smaller accounts were emptied."

"Why didn't you tell me this yesterday?"

"I wasn't getting arrested for murder yesterday. It wasn't me. I didn't kill anyone, and I know nothing about Copeland."

The interview carried on a while longer, and at the conclusion even Grant had to admit that he thought Whyte to be very convincing and released him without charge from the cells complex.

After he had left the station, Grant turned to Stuart and asked," Who the fuck is this guy, Neilson, then?"

"It's a long story, Davie, and I really can't tell you anything more. When it's all done and dusted, we'll have a pint or two."

Chapter Twenty-Four

The following day after Stuart had applied for and been granted a warrant to search Neilson's home address, the other members of Operation Iago and a search team arrived at his house. Forcing entry, they soon realised that the house looked like it had just been left, almost as if the occupier would return at any minute. Clothes were in wardrobes, food in the cupboards, and electrical items were still plugged into sockets. They knew, however, that the occupier was no longer at home and hadn't been seen for several days.

They spent the rest of the day in the house searching every nook and cranny in relation to the new information they had obtained from the Whyte interviews. Stuart had told the search team POLSA that he was specifically looking for details of bank accounts or any item pertaining to their use.

During the course of the day, they had turned up several bank statements, details of other accounts, and a card reader, all of which were seized for further examination. The computer in the house was also taken. As the house search drew to a close, the area outside the house was also searched and, after emptying the rubbish wheelie bin, the search teams found documentation in relation to one of their key information points that Stuart had outlined. Torn up into many pieces was an electricity bill and a phone bill in the name of Steven Randall, with a stated address at Upper Grove Street in Edinburgh. Painstakingly laid out on the kitchen table so that the details could be read, Jim Wilkinson had used his mobile phone to take a photograph of the reconstituted paperwork.

Inside the garden shed, one of the search team had found an old pair of black boots, with a distinctive tread pattern of a large, circular "whorl" at the ball of each foot. Having been told that

Neilson's car had been recovered in a dusty garage, he had asked if the boots could be the ones which had made the patterns in the dust when the car had been discovered. He shouted Collins over. Collins looked at the tread pattern and thought that they could be the same. Taking the knotted piece of string that Stuart had given him, he measured the sole of the boot against the string. They were the same size.

Not the greatest forensic examination ever done but a good indication that they could be onto a good thing, he thought to himself.

"Take them. We'll get them examined properly against the photographs," he instructed.

When they left the premises after several hours, the door was secured and the keys taken with them. Leaving a note on the kitchen table with details of what had happened should the occupier return, and an entry was placed on police command and control systems highlighting where they keys would be located.

Collins, Beattie, Wilkinson, and Reynold returned to their office and began pouring over what they had taken. The computer would be sent for examination by their experts in the hope that computerised bank transactions could be recovered, but they all knew that the details of the accounts that they now had, including those in Whyte's ledgers, would have to be progressed by obtaining permission to examine them from the banks concerned and that would require more warrants to be applied for. They worked long into the night preparing the application forms with details of the evidence that would substantiate their reasons for making the applications.

At two am they called it a day, or night as was the case, and decided that Steven Randall could wait until the morning when the offices that they needed to speak to were open once again.

After only a few hours' sleep, they were back at it again in the morning. Willie Stuart contacted the office informing them that Whyte's alibi had been checked out and he had indeed been at home when the gas man had called.

"We're still looking for our killer and Copeland's killer," he said in a phone call to Collins. "How'd you get on yesterday?"

Collins went on to explain what they had managed to secure. They had completed all the bank warrant applications and they had an address for Steven Randall.

"We found a pair of boots that look like the impressions in the dust at the garage. We've got them and they're being looked at right now," he said.

"They measured up against the bit of string?" Stuart enquired.

"Spot on, in my opinion, Willie."

"I know you'll do a good job, Shug. Keep at it" Stuart said.

With Jim Wilkinson back at the Buchan Murder Squad, Collins, Beattie, and Reynold busied themselves with the matter at hand, namely finding Steven Randall and who owned the address for the utility bills they had found. During the course of the day, they researched the address through the Register of Sasines and learned the owner of the property in Upper Grove Street was a Mohammed Rasul. He couldn't be found on any of the social media sites.

Using the photograph of the bills that Wilks had obtained and shared with them, they contacted the electricity company and the phone company and, after explaining the nature of their enquiry in half-truths, they were told that Steven Randall had not been a customer long, only a few months, in fact. The bills were sent out to the address and were not paid by direct debit.

"Why would Steven Randall's bill be in Dick Neilson's house, then? Is he renting Upper Grove Street? Or is it a pal of his?" Collins asked when they came together at lunchtime to swap information and hopefully gain a few ideas.

"Why don't we ask the neighbours? They might know Randall or who the landlord is. This guy Rasul owns it, but is he a landlord? It might even be let through an agency," Reynold had suggested.

"Did you check out Neilson's address with the Sasines?" Beattie asked.

"No. Should I have?"

"I don't know but it's just a thought. There might be some connection with Randall."

After lunch, Collins logged back into the internet and discovered that Neilson's address had recently been sold back to a building society for £175,000. Checking back through the records, he noted that Neilson had not had a mortgage for the property and it appeared that he had been given the house many years before. The sale date was a few months before Buchan had been shot.

"He must be living there as a lift tenant, rent free. When he's dead, the building society would then have the asset," Collins said to Beattie. "Let's go to the Upper Grove Street and ask a few questions."

The addresses in Upper Grove Street in the Fountainbridge area of Edinburgh consisted of tenement flats, three to a floor, and with three storeys. Sandstone build many years before, it was a popular area for students whilst studying in Edinburgh, due to it being near the city centre for all the bus routes, and, of course, the many pubs and clubs.

They found the flat easily but saw that it was nothing out of the ordinary, in common with most rented accommodations. They knocked on a few doors and asked several of the neighbours if they knew who the occupier was, where he was at present, or if they knew who rented out the flats. They checked the door jambs of the flat doors as, very often, with the number of times new tenants came to the flats, the postmen wrote the occupiers names there for future reference. They couldn't find Randall, however.

It was the occupants of the last house that they visited who suggested that they might try the letting agency on Morrison Street, as they dealt with several of the properties in the stair and, as far as they knew, several other occupiers of flats contacted them when something needed fixed. As Morrison Street was nearby, they called in there and made their enquiries.

After showing the letting agency staff their identification and explaining what they were after regarding their enquiry, they soon made some progress. The property, they knew, was owned by a Mohammed Rasul, or Rasul Mohammed. Did they let out any of his properties, particularly in Upper Grove Street?

"Yes, that's one of ours," the manager responded.

"We really need to see the documentation that you might have," Collins asked. "This is a serious enquiry and time is not on our side."

"Okay," she said. "Just wait and I'll have a look."

A few minutes later, she came back with a buff coloured folder and placed in on the table in front of her.

"Steven Randall. Yes, that's him. He took a year's lease on the property about five months ago. Paid cash up front. He gave us a couple of references and they came back all okay."

Hmm, Collins thought. *That'll be about the time he sold his own house and started pocketing Buchan's cash.*

"Did you deal with the let of the property?" he asked.

"Not me, personally. One of my colleagues did."

"Are they in today?"

"Yes, it was Julie, I think. You want to speak to her?"

"Please," Collins said, taking a photocopy of a photograph from inside his jacket.

When Julie came into the office, he quickly explained why he was there and asked her if the photograph was Steven Randall.

"Yes, that's him," came her very quick reply. "I remember him because he paid in cash. Six thousand pounds, including the deposit."

"Is it normal that cash is paid up front like that?" Beattie asked.

"It happens quite a lot with well-off parents from abroad paying for their kids for the year. Yes, it's not unusual," Julie replied.

Collins and Beattie looked at each other briefly, knowing what the other was thinking. Well, well, Dick Neilson had become Steven Randall and the photo was a copy of his warrant card image. Not strictly legal, they knew, but it had served its purpose.

Thanking them for their time and asking them to keep all the documents safe, Collins and Beattie left.

As they sat in their car, they talked over what they had learned. If Neilson was using a fake identity, he would have to be able to prove who he was, and he would therefore have to have some documentation to back up his story.

"What if he's changed his name legally? Can you do that quickly?" Beattie asked almost rhetorically.

"You must be. It looks like he's done it. Let's Google it and find out."

After a few minutes on their phones, they quickly learned that the process was simple, in hindsight, very obvious, and entirely legal.

In Scotland, unlike the rest of the United Kingdom, any person could make a Statutory Declaration to the Registrar of Scotland that they wanted to change their name. This could be done once in a calendar year for a forename and up to three times for a surname. All that was required was that the relevant application form be completed and countersigned by a solicitor, notary, or any other suitably qualified person. No reason had to be given for the change of name as long as the relevant fee was paid.

"Talk about hiding in plain sight," Collins said. "If he's done this, there'll be details of it recorded somewhere."

On their way back to the office, they swung by the Registrar of Scotland at the offices in Waterloo Place, immediately behind the statue of the Duke of Wellington sitting on his horse, Copenhagen. Once more, they explained to the staff who they were and what they were looking for and were soon directed to the appropriate archive. They knew that they only had to go back a few months to check for Richard Neilson or Steven Randall, and very quickly, they turned up what they hoped they would find. They read through the forms that had been submitted by Neilson changing his name to Steven Randall and, of course, saw his signature on the application form.

Taking a copy of Neilson's signature he had obtained from some Police documents that he had signed, Collins saw that it was a perfect match, at least to his untrained eye. Taking a photocopy of the declaration forms, they left the building and headed back to the office to update the others before contacting Stuart with their latest findings.

"Christ, that's clever and so obvious now," Stuart said, when told.

"Absolutely. Of course, he'll have had the notary countersignature bit done by a pal of his, or he's done it himself with his left hand or whatever, but that's not all."

"Oh, what else is there?"

"I would imagine that if he's changed his name, he'll have had to change his own bank details, too -- his passport, driving licence, etc. With the passport, he would be able to rent the flat at Upper Grove Street with no problem, and with his utility bills and all that, he could have opened up loads of other bank accounts. He's probably said his passport is lost or stolen, kept it, and asked for another in his new name. That might explain why he just disappeared like a fart in a hurricane. We'll have to check with the passport office when he changed them over. We know when Dick Neilson left the country, but we've been looking for him in Spain under the wrong name. Interpol should have been looking for Steven Randall. The border force systems might not have been updated quick enough to catch him leaving"

"Fuck, you're right. Can you follow that up in the morning and get a team together again to do the address at Upper Grove Street?" Stuart agreed.

"We've been doing that since we got back. With the money he got from the sale of his house and the cash he's stolen off Buchan, he's got an awful lot of spending money for his wee trip. The guys looking at the ledgers have just started, but there's a huge amount of money that's been planked away, Willie"

"How much are we talking about?"

"It's looking like there's going to be six zeros after the first number."

"So, it's millions, then?"

"A long way to go, but, aye, millions."

Chapter Twenty-Five

First thing the following morning, Reynolds made his way to the Procurator Fiscals offices at the city's Sheriff Court on Chamber Street in Edinburgh, where he made the formal application for a warrant to search the address at Upper Grove Street. As before, Collins and Beattie armed themselves and made contact with the Force search unit asking for a team to be ready and on standby for when Reynolds returned. It wasn't long before they were on the road, the search team having been briefed as to what the Operation Iago officers were looking for; specifically, a firearm and clothing, hopefully, and thereafter bank statements, card readers, and assorted financial details.

Approaching the flat from the south side and a short distance from the premises, they all entered the common stair as quietly and as inconspicuously as possible, given that several were dressed in their public order kit, carrying bags of equipment, whilst the others were dressed in their blue search overalls. They were not expecting anyone to be at home, after all. Entry was forced by use of the Hooli bar and single "bosh," causing a minimum of damage as the team rushed into the house. There was, indeed, no one at home in the small flat, which consisted of a living room, kitchen, one bedroom, and a bathroom.

The teams soon settled into their meticulous search procedures, looking for "voids" or apertures where anything could be hidden. This was different from a drug search, as small amounts of drugs were usually left out on open display, their users being too lazy to hide it away. It was only the dealers' notations that were hidden away, fearful of the consequences of having them found.

Sure enough, the teams proved their worth once more when the pair in the kitchen found a void at the rear of the kitchen. The work tops appeared to have had a second layer of waterproof sealant applied to the edges that joined them to the walls and the kick plates that clipped into place on the legs of the standing cupboards were noted to be loose. When they were removed, the officers saw that there was a gap which had been dug out of the masonry low down, level with the floor. A false skirting board had been placed in front of the gap, partially concealing what had been placed inside. With considerable difficulty and by using a wire coat hanger that had been straightened out to form a hook, the officers pulled out a black attaché-sized case with tan edges. Without touching it, they shouted for Collins and Beattie to come to them.

"Great work, boys" Collins beamed. "This is what we've been after for the last three or four weeks," he said, realising that it must contain the rifle that had killed Buchan and Copeland.

Putting on a pair of latex gloves, he clicked the locks on the case and found it to be open.

"Right enough. If he had stolen it, he wouldn't have the keys or the combination; would he?" he remarked to Beattie.

Opening the case, he saw the Blaser .308 rifle broken down into its component parts and all placed in their respective foam cut-out compartments.

"Bingo," Jamie said.

"Yup, jackpot," Shug confirmed, closing the case and inserting it into a large brown paper bag that would preserve any fingerprints on the outside of the case. Beattie and Collins noted on the log of the search who had found it and where it had been found before taking it out the room to allow the search to continue.

"Hang on, Shug," the search officer said, still lying on his back with his left arm under the cupboard units. "There's more," he said, trying to fish out some other items that his colleague could see by the light of his torch.

"Got it," he beamed, as he dragged a plastic pouch out from under the cupboard and a pair of black Altberg boots, covered in mud.

It was a small clear plastic bag with a zip-lock top, presumably to keep it safe from the damp conditions under the cupboard. With his latex-covered gloved hands, he gently lifted it by the edge and handed it up to Beattie. Inside the bag, he could see that there was a card reader of some type, with a slot to swipe a bank card. It was not at all like the card readers the banks used as an additional level of security. There were also what looked like blank cards with a magnetic strip down one side, bearing no details as to the account holders' names or the name of the bank.

"I think that that's a card scanner device," the cop who found it said to him. "You know, the type of thing that the fraudsters put on the bank ATMs to get card details from the folks taking out money. They get the account details from that and then, with a small camera alongside, they manage sometimes to get the PIN numbers from careless folk who don't hide their number when they're putting it in. These cards will be clones of the real ones."

"I think you're right, there," Collins agreed and then, as before, he bagged up the evidence.

The boots were placed in a large paper bag that would allow them to breathe and dry out. If anything fell off, it would be kept within the bag and could still be examined.

As the search progressed, the team found several utility bills, bank statements, and other documentation in the name of Steven Randall, as would be expected, and all of it was bagged up and retained for forensic investigation at a later time.

"Find!" came the shout from the bathroom. The pair searching there had discovered another hiding place under the shower unit, the side of which had been cut through with a small hand saw and then stuck back in place with waterproof silicone. The silicone had bled onto the linoleum flooring, something that any self-respecting plumber would never have done. Either that or he was just poor at his job. In any case, it had been an indication to the officers that something was not right. When the side casing had been removed, the officer inserted his hand and could feel a smooth, square object inside but again he was having difficulty in reaching it.

"Gimme that hook thing that you made up," he shouted through to his colleague and, with that, he was able to recover a small laptop computer, which was bagged up as before.

Bolstered by the finds they had made and very conscious of the fact that they were dealing with a very creative individual, the POLSA gathered the team together at the end of the search and asked them if they were sure they had covered everything they could think of. They had.

"Without taking this place apart – all the units off the walls and the floorboards up – I think that we've covered everything, Shug."

"Can you have a look at everything again? Just swap the teams over to double-check where the others have searched," Collins asked him.

The POLSA then re-allocated the pairs into different rooms and asked that they check all the fixtures and fittings for signs of having been tampered with. They rolled up the floor coverings and checked the flooring – just to be on the safe side – and, once completed, he pronounced himself satisfied that they had got everything.

"Fucking great job, lads," Collins said to the assembled teams. "I'm gonna be up to my arse in paperwork for the foreseeable future, but fucking great job. Thank you. Can you send me your statements on email when you get a chance?" he asked, and the nodded their co-operation.

After the search team left the flat, Collins, Beattie, and Reynolds waited for a joiner to come and repair the damaged lock, and, when completed, they dropped the new keys off with the letting agent they had spoken to the previous day, asking that should anyone call on them regarding the flat, to give them a call, too. They returned to Police HQ with the productions they had recovered.

On arrival back there, they made straight for McInnes' office and updated him with what they had found.

"You've got the rifle?" he asked, almost disbelieving them.

"Well, we've got a rifle. We think that it is the rifle, but forensics will have to confirm that."

"Right, then. No time like the present. Come with me," he said to Collin, as they both walked to the lifts. "And bring that with you," he said, pointing to the attaché case housing the rifle.

They went straight to the identification branch offices where McInnes spoke quietly with the officer in charge.

"I need this examined now, please. Drop everything. We think that this is the murder weapon for the Buchan and Copeland cases. If you get any fingerprints on it – anything – let me know before you go any further."

"Okay. Can do, Boss. You want it test fired so we can do the comparison with the two rounds recovered. Peter's still here?" Peter Lawson, the ballistic expert for the Force, had been on duty during the day and would now be working overtime into the evening to make the match, if possible.

"Yes. Overtime is not an issue. I need a result as soon as possible."

Although fingerprints can be lifted from rough surfaces, it is a much more difficult process, as the techniques involved require the use of a casting material that fills in the textured areas, allowing the whole print to be lifted. They cannot be lifted using normal aluminium powder and ordinary acetate plastic lifts.

Lawson decided that it would be better to use the chemical cyanoacrylate, or superglue, which he would cook in a Gallenkamp oven. With a little of the chemical placed onto a cotton ball alongside the attaché case and then heated in the humidifier, the proteins from the skin would react with the superglue and rapidly appear on the case.

Because it was superglue, the impression would be hardened against any rough treatment. It would be a simple process to add a fluorescent dye to highlight any prints found and then to photograph and, hopefully, identify them. If aluminium powder was applied, the prints could be destroyed, as the ultra-fine powder only fills in the gaps on the rougher surfaces of the case.

Taking the component parts from the case, he examined the rifle parts individually and while the case was "cooking" he looked for prints on the weapon using aluminium powder. There were two sets that he found which were viable on the butt section and one set on the barrel. He recovered all three and signed over the join between the lift and the acetate sheet of plastic that the lift was attached to. He would deal with that in due course.

Turning to the weapon itself, he joined the pieces together and took one of the bullets from the case, noting how many there were and testing them for fingerprints. He knew that he could do the rest at a later time.

Walking over to a large tank of water, eight feet long and three feet deep that had been built within the laboratory for the purpose of ballistic examination, Lawson shouted out "Big bangs" to the colleague that was assisting him, before loading the weapon and pointing the muzzle at the tank of water. He fired the weapon into the water. The loud report of the weapon was deafened by the soundproofing in the office and the sound-suppressing headsets that they wore, but it always came as a shock to the staff in offices nearby. The round tore through the water, leaving a trail of bubbles in its wake, but was slowed down in the water to such an extent that it remained undamaged and could be recovered from the tank for examination under his microscope. Taking large forceps, he recovered the round from the bottom of the tank.

Lawson spent the next few hours looking at the rounds recovered from the bodies of Buchan and Copeland, comparing the striation marks on each of the rounds with the ones he had fired into the water tank. In his opinion, they matched. He then examined the firing pin marks on the rear of the shell casing from the bullet he had fired with the one that had been recovered from the locus of Copeland's murder and, again, in his opinion, they matched. They had the murder weapon. His findings would have to be double-checked, of course.

It was late into the evening when the attaché case in the Gallenkamp oven was ready and, sure enough, the fingerprint impressions were visible. He added a fluorescent dye to highlight them against the tan colour of the case, photographed them, and then completed his day's work by examining the bullets held within the attaché case.

He found several finger impressions and was able to photograph them, too. As he had been told to recover the prints only and thereafter wait for further instruction, he decided to secure everything he had found in a locked facility within the lab, then wrote up his findings and emailed them to McInnes. When finished, he felt like his eyes were staring out of his head, and he knew that he was finished for the day. Any more, and he knew he would make mistakes.

I think he'll be a happy man tomorrow, he said to himself, thinking about McInnes.

When he opened up his emails the following morning, McInnes was indeed happy to see that there had been prints found on the weapon, but he knew that without an identification, it would have been a pointless operation. He immediately went up to the ID branch offices where he spoke with Peter Lawson again and asked him to check the fingerprints held on file for Dick Neilson, first and foremost, and then Howard Whyte. As a belt and braces double-check, to run them through the computer database.

It took a few hours of work given the number of prints that he had recovered from the case, the rifle, and the bullets, but he was able to make matches for Neilson on the case and on the rifle butt and, in the case of Howard Whyte, on some of the rounds that had been in the case. He phoned McInnes when he had completed his work and informed him.

"Excellent work, Peter. Thank you for your efforts, but keep the information to yourself for now. Could you get the results double-checked but don't tell them whose print our main man is?"

"No problem, Boss. I'll get on it right away, and we can have the paperwork with you later in the morning"

"Lovely. Thanks again.

Chapter Twenty Six

The Dark Web of the internet is very complex, although easily accessed through software designed to enable confidential and anonymous communications. These programmes enable friend-to-friend file sharing or total privacy when browsing the internet on the pages of the "Dark Market" for illegal materials or activities, such as the purchase of controlled drugs, terrorism, counterfeited or illegally obtained credit card and bank account information, or forged documents.

The programmes use what is termed an "Onion Network," where the technology employed encrypts the users' data through layers and layers of separate and individual servers, thus protecting identification and guaranteeing anonymity. As a result, the sender of any information remains anonymous because each intermediary in the chain only knows the location of the previous and following servers. The "Dark Market" employs Bitcoins, a cryptocurrency, as the payment for these services and can be transferred into any currency throughout the world. It has been estimated that upwards of six million individual users conduct their illegal business in this manner.

That certainly was the case as the police computer experts got to work on the hard drives that the Operation Iago officers had recovered from Whyte and the two computers recovered from Neilson's home address as well as from Upper Grove Street. Some of the information was recoverable, such as the internal transfers from bank to bank, or from account to account, that were found on Whyte's computer. That information could be used to trace the flow of money from the street drugs dealings.

However, Neilson had downloaded a "Tor" encryption programme to mask his dealings and, as a result, they could only find the server following and which thereafter became and remained anonymous. Nevertheless, the experts recovered as much information as they could and completed their reports and statements as DI Stuart had requested.

A few days later, Willie Stuart and Davie Grant joined McInnes in his office for a briefing of the current status of their respective cases. Over a cup of coffee at the large conference table, they shared their information and ideas as to how to progress. After explaining to Davie Grant the secret nature of Stuart's secondary enquiry into Neilson's corrupt activities, which had now been confirmed, McInnes asked for Stuart's summary of the circumstances.

"As it stands right now," Willie started, "we've got Neilson's prints on a glass pick-out from the HB in Hawick, where the Blaser rifle was stolen. We know he was shooting with the complainer who had the rifle stolen. He'll have to explain that, although we will have some tap dancing to do in order to explain how we identified him."

"Tap dancing like Gene Fucking Kelly, Willie," McInnes suggested.

"Yeah, okay. All the fingerprint evidence that we have against him comes from the prints that were taken when he joined and not as a convicted person. We can't lead with that in court. But we also have him in images from the street CCTV on the night that

Buchan was shot. It's not great evidence, but it'll help. I think that is what might have spooked him into leaving so quickly. He's seen himself in the images and thought that we would make the connection quicker that we did. He was right, of course. We didn't see it at all." He paused to see if either of the two in the room wanted to pass a comment. They didn't.

"We made the connection to him through the green Fiesta car that was seen near to the Buchan locus and traced it back to his mother's address in Musselburgh. She still owns the house and is in a home with Alzheimer's, so there's no point in speaking to her at all. That's when I had the argument with him. The tread pattern on the boots we found at Randall's/Neilson's flat match the footprints in the dust at the garage in Musselburgh. The mud and shite on them match the mud on the pedals from the car and on the mats.

"Via the mobile phones, we traced Howard Whyte, the book keeper, and he told us everything he knew, eventually. It now seems that Neilson has used a card swipe on the bank cards that Whyte had in the plastic sleeves in his folders. The ones with the bank details and PIN numbers. It looks like he's swiped the cards when Whyte wasn't looking and just noted the PIN numbers from the folder. He's then created the cloned cards from the stuff he's got off the Dark Web and then filled his boots with everyone's money. He then fucked off to Tenerife under his own name but has very obviously got another false identity or two up his sleeve. I asked Interpol to check for Neilson and Randall in Spain, but I'm not holding out much hope of his being traced or found under these details."

Again, he paused to see if anyone had any questions.

"How do you know about the cards being swiped, and I don't mean stolen?" Davie Grant asked.

"Neilson's fingerprints were found on the plastic sleeves and on some of the bank cards. They wouldn't be there for any other reason. He should never have handled the folders, according to Whyte, unless he was up to no good. Besides, apart from his prints being on the plastic sleeves, they're also on the bank cards and are always at the opposite end from the magnetic strip, indicating that they had been swiped. His prints are obviously on the rifle, and the rifle was used to shoot Buchan. The test firing proved that beyond doubt."

"How are you getting on with tracing all these bank accounts from the students that went home or whatever?" McInnes asked.

"Slowly. We've had three guys looking at the books and even Whyte's been in to give them a hand with it. He's desperate to curry favour and impress the judge with his helping us. There's a lot of money involved. Somewhere in the region of one-point-five million pounds."

"One and a half million quid? That's what he's got away with?" McInnes asked, whistling after he said it.

"It's in that ballpark, yes. But it's been put through so many accounts by Whyte and then transferred into the Steven Randall accounts, somewhere that we haven't found yet. My guess is that Neilson will have further identities that he's used and is still using. I don't think we'll ever learn how many he's got and which he's using. You can buy fake IDs off the internet."

"What about you, Davie?"

"Pretty much the same as Willie, to be honest. We don't have any CCTV or witnesses. We have the shell casing at the locus but that's got Whyte's fingerprints on it. To be fair, his prints are on more of the bullets that Willie's boys got back from Upper Grove Street, and it seems to be just like he explained when he was interviewed. That, and the fact that he was at home when the gas man called and so couldn't have been there when Copeland was shot. There's no forensic evidence available, either."

"Why would he shoot Copeland?" McInnes asked.

"Maybe to muddy the water for us? Get us thinking that it was the Southside who done him in? Point the finger at someone else long enough for him to get the hell out of Dodge? If that was his intention, he did a good job of it," Grant said, looking for suggestions and explanations, as well.

"I think he's done in Buchan as a result of his being blackmailed, and then he's thought that if he was to steal his money and cover his tracks, we couldn't find it or him. You know as well as I do that it's hard enough to trace money through the banking systems when someone is still alive, but when they're dead and we're dealing with executors of their estate, it makes it so very much more difficult." The two other detective nodded at Stuart's summary of the situation.

"Where do we go from here, then?" McInnes asked.

"Well, I'm satisfied that we have our man," Stuart said in a matter of fact way. "We'll obviously keep on examining the computers and try to follow the money and the identities as best we can. But, as you well know, it's gonna be a bastard to unravel."

"Me, too," Davie Grant chipped in. "In the absence of anything else that we've so far uncovered, and to be honest it's not a lot, I think that Nielson is our boy. He's certainly our best shot – if you'll excuse the pun."

"Alright, then," McInnes said "Your squad has been running for a couple of months now, Willie. Scale it back and tie up any loose ends that you might have. Take all the enquiries that you have on-going to a logical conclusion and write up what you have. Davie, can you do the same. There may be little point, but check with the passport office for Neilson's and Randall's passport number going through any airport, including international, if you can. We need to find this double murderer and get him brought back."

Chapter Twenty Seven

Although McInnes had instructed the SIOs of the Buchan and Copeland squads to scale back the enquiry and thereafter report the facts and circumstances to the Crown Office, the enquiry into Buchan's murder was a long way from being completed. The computer experts who tried to decipher the information contained within Neilson's and Whyte's computers had many avenues to follow, given the amount of bank account sorting codes and account numbers that had been input over the last few years.

Although Whyte continued to assist with the enquiry -- and this aspect proved far less challenging -- the ledgers were eventually unravelled and a report prepared in a well-structured and concise manner. This would later be used to instigate proceeding under the Proceeds of Crime Act in an effort to have the money that Buchan had concealed throughout his supposedly legitimate business confiscated.

The computers that Neilson had used became a painstaking business, especially in light of his encryption programmes. Bank warrants were executed against all of the accounts that they knew of, in the hope that the respective banks would have details of where any money had been transferred to, but everything ended up pointing to that of Steven Randall and the accounts that he held at branches of various banks.

Following the money trail, the financial investigations team that had been formed to track it down found that the trail ran cold after it was uncovered that huge amounts of money had been transferred to various banks in Tenerife such as Santander, Caixa Bank, Banca March, and Deutsche Bank. They would have no jurisdiction in Spain and, in any case, they knew that the money would be gone by the time they got around to convincing Interpol to act on their behalf. Interpol never did find Neilson or Randall in Spain.

While this work was ongoing, Collins, Beattie, and Reynold attended to all the phone records that they had applied for and, yet again, it took considerable time to match up each number to a name and thereby prove the association which would assist in the POCA asset confiscation process. The one piece of useful evidence that they did turn up was a mobile phone contact from one of the banks. When Neilson had stolen Whyte's bank security card reader, he had had to change the phone contact details in order to update new payee information from each account he had accessed.

When a new payee was input on internet banking, the card relating to the account was put into the reader and the PIN number inserted. An automated service then called back with a reciprocal number that had to be input into the reader. This helped to prove that Neilson had taken the money and that Whyte had been duped. The new payees related to Steven Randall's accounts once more but the phone number was Neilson's personal phone.

Months overdue by the time the evidence was available with which to prosecute him, Whyte was reported for his money laundering offences by Jim Wilkinson and due consideration was given to the fact that he had been a considerable help to the enquiry. He would later serve a year in prison.

Willie Stuart prepared his report into the killing of Matthew Buchan and the internal corruption case against Neilson at the same time. What else could he do, apart from report the facts as he knew them and how they had come into his knowledge? It would be up to the Force to decide how they wanted to handle the fallout from the case at a future time.

Apart from anything else, there were the two cops who had been hiding the intelligence reports along with Neilson to be dealt with, but rather than wait on all the subsidiary enquiries to be completed, he wrote out what he knew to be true at that time and added appendices as they became available. The collation of the many, many statements that had been taken from witnesses and the police officers involved – the ID branch, search teams, members of the shoot in Hawick who had assisted Collins, old folks home staff – all had to be gathered. This was a task for a squad in and of itself, but Stuart waded through it alone and eventually completed it.

"What's going to happen now then, Boss?" he said, as he handed a bound copy to McInnes. "I've got it on email that I can send you, but I'm old-school and like to have a hard copy in my hand."

"The Crown Office is aware of what's happened. I'm sure you know that. I think that they'll issue a warrant for his arrest in the event that he's found, wherever that may be. If there's a warrant for his arrest, he better be squeaky clean, 'cause he's fucked if he ever gets arrested."

"That's a small satisfaction, if I'm truthful, Boss. I'd really like to get my hands on him."

"I know, Willie. I know you would. We all would, but you know how it goes. Sometimes you win, sometimes you lose," he said, knowing well the deflated feelings his DI was now experiencing.

"Get yourself away with your team, have a good night out, and know that you did a good job. And you have done a bloody good job."

Stuart left McInnes' office having already made arrangements for them to have an end-of-squad night out to celebrate the end of their association. All five of the Operation Iago team members went out for a meal and several pints to celebrate the end of their long and sometimes arduous journey together. They were dropped off in Edinburgh's High Street and made for Gordon's Trattoria, a restaurant frequented by many police and detective officers over the years, often whilst they were still on duty.

Taking a table at the rear of the premises, they ate and drank for several hours, enjoying each other's company. They all preferred to stay where they were rather than move on to a pub where it would be busy and they couldn't get seats. The manager of the restaurant didn't mind, either, as they were spending a load of money on beer and wine.

It was well into the evening when they were all the worse for wear that Stuart bumped into an old associate in the toilets. As he stood at the urinal with his head against the wall in front of him to stop himself from swaying, with disastrous consequences for his shoes and trousers, he heard, "Hello, Mr Stuart."

Turning to his right and trying to focus, he looked at Ryan Docherty.

"Hello there, Ryan. What are you doing here?"

"Just in for something to eat with the wife, Mr Stuart. How are you?"

"A bit pished, if I'm honest, Ryan. A little bit pished."

"So I see. What's the occasion?"

"We've just finished the enquiry we were on. You know who I mean?"

"Aye, I know who you mean. Did you solve it?"

Despite his drunken condition, Stuart was aware of his surroundings and who he was speaking to, and he suddenly had an idea.

"Ryan, can I speak with you outside and away from prying ears?"

"I'm not going to tell you anything else, Mr Stuart. I'm really not"

"No, no. I want to tell you something, Ryan, something that might be to your advantage. I'm going out for a smoke. I'll see you out front in a few minutes."

"Aye, okay, then," Docherty replied, slightly confused.

On returning to his table, Stuart sat for a few minutes and watched as Docherty passed their table. No one in the company looked as if they had recognised him. *Must only be me, then,* he thought to himself. Not even Reynolds, who, to be fair, was half asleep with his head on his chest.

"I'm going out for a fag. Back shortly, chaps. You coming for a blaw, Shug? Carry on, chaps," he said in mock military jargon, complete with accent, before he and Collins made their way to the front door. At the space reserved outside the restaurant for smoking, the cold night air made them shiver as they left. He saw Docherty standing there, also smoking.

"So, Mr Stuart, what can you do for me?" he said, half smiling.

Stuart looked back into the restaurant and saw that he was out of the line of sight of his table. He saw that they were alone in the smoking area.

"Ryan, this is a colleague of mine. Shug, this is Ryan, an old adversary."

Collins nodded at Docherty, remembering him from when he had searched his house and found the SIM card and notebook all those months before.

"We know who killed Matty but we're never going to get him. We don't know where he is. There's a case against him right now and a warrant will be issued for his arrest, but I don't think that it'll ever be enforced."

"For fuck's sake, Willie," Collins protested.

"How's that?" Docherty asked, ignoring Collins comment.

"He fucked off to Spain under a different name, and he's got loads of other names that we don't know about. I won't tell you how we know, but we know that he's done it."

"Aye, go on," Ryan encouraged him.

Stuart took a drag on his fag and inhaled.

"Richard Neilson or Steven Randall is all I know. Left for Tenerife about a month after your boss got shot. I know that you and Matty were pretty close. Perhaps you could use the information, if you want to, of course."

"Is this a wind-up or are you just fishing for information? The Polis telling me who they're after?"

"Straight up, Ryan. Check it out with Knuckles if you don't believe me. I've done my job. Done my duty. Do what you want with the information. That's me finished with it. I'm going back to my table, and I'm gonna finish my drinks and go home."

"Okay, Mr Stuart. Cheers."

"Willie, you know that you just might've signed his death warrant?" Collins said after Docherty had gone back inside.

"But if you lay down with dogs, you'll get up with fleas. Do you have any issue with telling Doc?"

"Seeing as you mention it, no, not really. I hope he gets his just rewards right enough."

Chapter Twenty Eight

The hugely profitable trade in cocaine from South America, where it is almost exclusively grown from the coca plant, refined and manufactured into its powder form, is constantly evolving as the authorities adapt and improve their counter-strategies to the cartels' illegal shipments. Since the demise of Pablo Escobar and his Columbian monopoly of the trade, there is now a competitive market, with many countries like Peru, Bolivia, and Ecuador all producing supplies for the cartels to exploit.

The rise of the Mexican organisations, such as the Juarez cartel, the Tijuana cartel, or the Gulf cartel has filled the void, but, as a result, they have also come into conflict with the Colombian Norte del Valle and AUC (United Self-Defence Force of Colombia) as they vie for supremacy. This has created a huge increase in violent crime in Mexico, particularly in gruesome and horrific killings of people involved in the trade, to serve as a warning to others. It has been estimated that over 164,000 people had been murdered in the previous decade.

Moving their goods overland into Brazil, the main point of shipment to Europe due to its geographical position of being only 1800 miles from the coast of West Africa, the Mexican cartels move the cocaine onwards by various means, either through the preferred shipping route or through the air. Container ships are now more prevalent due to the amount that can be moved at one time, and the cartels exploit the political unrest and poverty in the West African states with substantial bribes to officials.

With a container identified within the port of exit, the cocaine shipment is secreted within a load of goods such as meat, fruit, or other foodstuffs, which are usually expedited through the port of entry due to their perishable nature. The only difficulty in this process, apart from being caught, is that the container has to be easily identifiable at both ports, as its registered number would become lost in the vast numbers that are brought into any freighting port.

With the officials and other authorities having been paid off at the entry port, tons of illegal drugs can be moved at one time, through container ports like Valencia in Spain, Lagos in Nigeria, Abidjan in Ivory Coast, or Tangier in Morocco. This method is known as "Rip on/Rip Off," referring, ironically, to the security seal that is attached to each container to show that it has not been tampered with. Unsurprisingly, those in control of the operations have sophisticated communications with each other and have connections and associates, known only to them, across the world in many organised crime groups in Europe, Africa, the United States and the Far East.

Whilst he was never going to move in such high circles, Ryan Docherty had his connections, too, in towns like Liverpool, Manchester, and Glasgow and it was through these connections that he put the word out that he was looking for an individual called Richard Neilson or Steven Randall, a Scotsman who had been a cop, and who had disappeared in Tenerife, Spain after stealing a lot of money from his organisation.

He outlined that he would pay well for any information that would lead him to where he could be found and, never turning their respective noses up at the chance to make some money, the organisations across the globe spread the news by word of mouth and through phone calls. Many, if not all of the organisations, had diverse interests, as they were not averse to little assassination, for the right price.

In his own world, Docherty was well-placed to take over from Buchan. He knew the business well -- knew the contacts and the contracts -- and moved himself into the shoes that Buchan had left behind, employing the same means as Buchan had done all those years before. The template had been well-used and it served its purpose once again.

The drug war that Neilson had hoped to start never really materialised following Copeland's death. After his conversation with Stuart and Collins, he was smart enough to broker a deal with the Northsiders and establish who would be dealing in which area of the city, and they reached an agreement that they would not impinge upon each other's business interests. They were all keen not to bring the full attention of the police down on them in a crackdown of biblical proportions and, as time passed, each side settled down into their respective trades with new bosses at the helm.

It was over a year later when he was contacted by an associate in Manchester with some information that might be of interest to him. As a major supplier of cocaine and heroin to the United Kingdom, his network connections had fed back to him details about a man living in Cancun, Mexico who was known to get drunk regularly and had begun to shout his mouth off about how much money he had stashed away following his shady dealings back in Scotland. The contact in Mexico, connected to the Gulf cartel who operated out of Matamoros, near the border with Texas in the United States, had done and said nothing, preferring to wait for further instructions before acting.

"Do you have a photograph of him?" Docherty had been asked.

"No, I don't but if you check the newspapers, you'll see him there. There's a warrant for his arrest that was circulated. He might be on the Interpol website, too."

"What do you want done, if it's him, Ryan?"

"I want him ended. How much, though?"

"I'll get back to you with a price, but it'll be cheaper seeing as it's in Mexico. There's plenty of people over there willing to do the work. The going rate is about twenty thousand U.S. dollars. That's about fifteen grand over here."

"That'll work," Docherty replied.

"Usual means of payment, plus my commission?

"No problem. Cheers"

In order to enter Mexico, a traveller must complete a single entry visa on their arrival and this can be upgraded to a temporary residence visa, provided the required fee and documentation is provided. This would allow a traveller to remain in the country for between three months and four years, as long as evidence is provided that they are self-sufficient and can show investments or a bank balance of at least 62,000 pounds and monthly income of 1,300 pounds.

With the money that he had been earning whilst with the police, the sale of his house, and the proceeds of his thefts, Neilson had no trouble in doing that. The investment portfolio that he had accrued in the British Virgin Islands, where limited tax was paid across the board, made him a rich man even before he had stolen the money from Buchan.

After he had flown to Tenerife, he had transferred Buchan's cash into the accounts of Steven Randall and immediately transferred them to the accounts he had opened and held there. After his hurried departure, he had not had the time or opportunity to tie up the loose ends that he knew he had left behind, but he figured that he had covered his tracks well enough and by the time the authorities got around to chasing him, he would be long gone.

As was always the case, there were things that he knew he could have done better and things that had gone wrong. His "chance" meeting with Whyte had been engineered by him, of course, and it was always his intention of planting the rifle at his house. Except Whyte never left it to afford him the opportunity. He was similarly unable to dispose of the blank cards and card swipe that he had used to steal Buchan's money and thereby hopefully frame Whyte in Buchan's eyes.

But Buchan had found out that he was having dealings with Whyte and, knowing that Buchan wanted to keep everyone separate and isolated within his organisation, Neilson knew he was in trouble. He also found out through the police grapevine about the cop from the Scottish Crime Squad who was thought to be getting close to Buchan when he had heard McInnes speaking on the phone to the squad. Neilson knew that Buchan would come after him and decided to act first.

After emptying his Spanish accounts and transferring the proceeds contained within them to his British Virgin Island accounts, he had flown to Madrid, under his new identity obtained from the dark web via his remaining laptop computer that travelled with him. From Madrid, he crossed the Atlantic to Mexico City and then connected to Cancun. In due course, as a temporary resident, he had bought a plush apartment in a new development in Puerto Cancun, near the hotel district, with its many shops, attractions, and bars. Settling into his new life, he moved in a girlfriend to live with him, who was only too happy to indulge his sexual appetite in return for an affluent lifestyle. With very little to do to keep his mind occupied, he began to drink too much, too often.

In the company of many American business men who holidayed in the resort, it had been on one of these nights when he had spoken too loudly within earshot of several locals about his tax evasion and shady dealings with some underworld characters back home in Scotland, in an effort to impress his new friends, who had regaled him with their similar stories.

After eighteen months of enjoying the highlife in the warmth of the tropics, as a supposedly respectable businessman, he was walking back to his apartment with his girlfriend, both dressed in shorts and a T-shirt, when car drew up alongside them. Neilson looked to his left and saw that the driver was facing straight ahead as he slowed down on the approach to the traffic lights as they changed to red. They walked on towards the junction when, from the rear of the car, he saw the barrel of the Mac 10 machine pistol protruding from the open window.

Notoriously inaccurate, the Mac 10 magazine held either thirty or a hundred rounds and had a firing rate of 1200 9-millimeter rounds per minute. Neilson and his girlfriend were caught in the hail of bullets fired from the rear seat. At such close range, the sound suppressor did its job of masking the noise for those inside the vehicle. For Neilson, it was a different matter. He and his girlfriend heard nothing as the rapid fire of the weapon spewed out burning hot rounds into his body, knocking them both backwards against the wall of the building, their bodies shaking and bucking as round after round struck home. The last thing he experienced was the taste his own blood. As he started to fall, the continued spray from the Mac 10 caught them both in the head – once, twice, three times -- and they died instantly, shaking violently on the pavement. Although he didn't see it, the gunman got out the car and gave a short burst at point blank range to each of their heads and then calmly walked back to the car and was driven off.

His death didn't even make the news in Mexico, let alone internationally, but it was a few months later that Docherty was informed of his contract having been fulfilled. He paid the fee that was required and felt an inner satisfaction that his friend, Matty, had been avenged and that he had "broken his cherry" by ordering his first killing.

Of course, he would never, and could never, talk or say anything about it, as that would land him in a world of shite. But he knew that Willie Stuart had recognised that he had the balls to get it done. He wouldn't have passed on the information otherwise, would he?

Printed in Great Britain
by Amazon